# The Rut

# Also by Bernard Amador

*To Know Å Fallen Angel:*
*Understanding the Mind of a Sexual Predator*
*Cyber-Eugenics: The Neural Code*

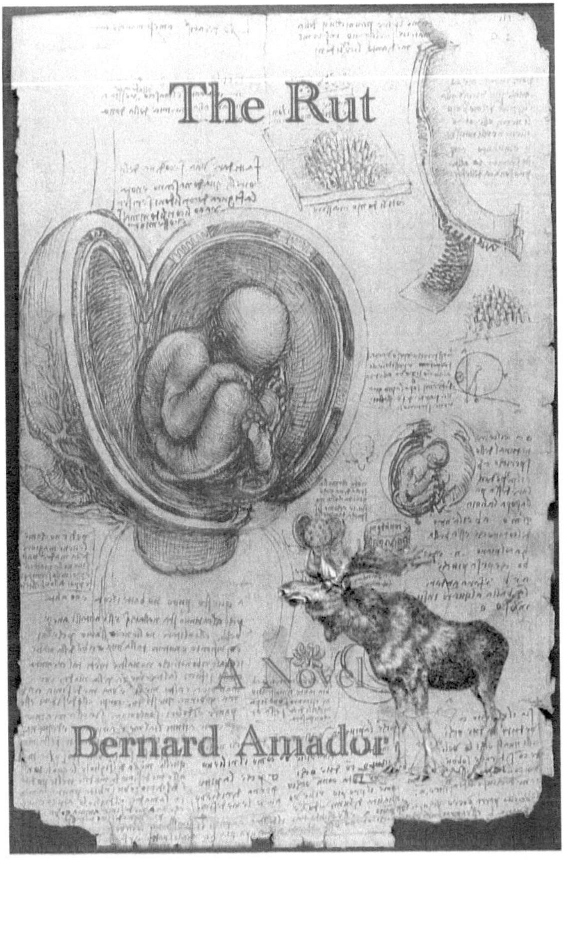

# The Rut

A Novel

Bernard Amador

## Hudson Mohawk Press
Latham, NY

Hudson Mohawk Press
595 New Loudon Road #138
Latham, New York 12110

www.hudsonmohawkpress.com

ISBN 978-0-984304028

Library of Congress Control Number:  2010921350

*Book design by Bernard Amador*

Cover Image: *Embryo in Uterus* by Leonardo da Vinci

Printed in the United States

# For Bill & Cuchie

**Thanks for sharing the inception of "The Rut".
Just remember:**

"If the rules tell us that we have to gain a full
understanding of fiction before we can write it
well, many of us will never pick up a pen"

—   Ellen J. Langer

# Contents

# Prologue

*Mooers, New York*
*October 23rd*

*T*here goes *l'orignal. That's what French Canadians call the moose. He's still looking with the desire to engage in the most important act of God, creation. I can remember the first time I learned what it was all about. We won't go there now. What I do know is that through it, I acquired the desire to design and bring into life something new. Being gay it seems I am predisposed to have a strong desire to create, whether making curtains for our new home or writing this book. It also seems that the desire to create life grows stronger as I age, wanting to have a new part of me I can nurture and watch grow. My problem is not that I am a gay man, no, that is not an obstacle. What blocks me from my natural urge to propagate is that I am in a relationship with Ean. Ean does share my desire to have a child. Having a child* *that is not biologically his own is not the path he wishes to be on. I chose it for him. Is it fate perhaps? My course in life is to partake in the continuous repetition of God's design, to engage in a fixed mode of procedure, a lesson in life that brings both moments of pain and joy to those who partake in the most crucial act of nature. I once partook of such action on a dare that resulted in life while trying to be accepted by others. But God took all that away from me. I now make the conscious decision to participate in the act of adoption. I also ask myself is my fate the result of the fact that I am aware of my own existence? Should I make the choice to bring forth action that results in a product of myself to be a part of this world? Being fully aware only allows me a certain level of control, a fraction of my destiny. I am powerless. I now know that it is the creator and ruler of the universe who presides over the course of worldly affairs. Over and over the creator gives me the same thought that takes a routine synaptic path channeling the idea driven by the sexual excitement that such thoughts bring into being. The result is not what I had in mind; it is the consequence of a greater creator who leads me to these pages to share with you a report of the facts concerning the matter in question, "The Rut".*

# Part I

# Adoption

# Chapter I

## L'orignal

"Come to bed!"

It is late and Ean is not asleep. He called. I can tell when he's signaling to mate.

"I'll be there soon!"

I put down my pen and left the nursery to answer his call. Like any good mate, I answered his, performed my duty, and returned to the nursery when he fell asleep. We had to get to work in the morning but I wanted to get a few more words written before the weekend was over. I picked up my pen. Ean did not know that since its inception I had started documenting our idea to adopt the child and what we were about to undertake that coming week. I sat in the chair at the desk in our new nursery and stared at the photos that the child's mother had sent me. My vision was all so clear.

*L'orignal* bolted across Interstate-87 as he heard a truck's horn blow as it approached. He made his way to safety. The loud honk blew a second time as the moose ran off the side of the road and into the brush. Ean could not hear it in the distance as he turned off the shower and pulled back its curtain. His tall lanky body stepped out onto the bathroom rug. His wet olive skin glistened. Ean ran both hands back over his shimmering black hair as water streamed behind his ears. A few seconds later he could hear the echo of the moose's call. Ean is what they call an early riser. The sound of the truck horn blew a third time as he reached for his towel and dried off as he pressed his feet into the bathroom rug to absorb the water. The mist of the shower fogged up the window as he wiped his body dry, and wiped the glass to look outside. It was still dark. Ean could not see a thing. There was a mist in the air. It was late October and the mornings were getting colder. Fall was here. Ean dreaded this time of year but welcomed the bright reds, oranges, yellows, greens, and browns that the season offered. It was five thirty in the morning. He walked out of the bathroom and into our master suite. I was still snuggled in bed hugging my pillow as Ean dried his hair. He walked slowly towards me and reached for the lamp near my side of the bed and turned it on. I did not flinch. With towel in hand Ean gently touched my arm curled around the pillow to wake me.

"Sweetie, it's time to get up."

I hugged the pillow tighter and nestled my face into it.

"Hey, it's time to get up," said Ean as the alarm clock went off.

I let go of the pillow and turned my body towards the alarm clock that sat on the night stand. Just a few hours earlier I had closed my journal with Da Vinci's *Studies of Embryos* on the cover and pulled the elastic strap from behind it and placed the journal in the drawer.

I shut off the alarm clock and pursed my lips in Ean's direction. Ean kissed me as I turned away and climbed out of the bed and headed for the bathroom.

"We're getting closer to the big day," I said.

"You don't have to remind me," said Ean as I disappeared into the bathroom.

As I showered, Ean entered the bathroom, hung up his towel and returned to the bedroom to finish dressing. After he dressed he went into the kitchen to make a pot of coffee. This was a routine that would soon be changing. After Ean filled the coffee pot with water and poured ground coffee into the top of the machine, he turned on the power button to begin the brewing process. He could hear the machine begin to percolate as he entered the spare bedroom. He loved our camp. But would he love it more with the addition? The room brightened as he turned on the light switch. Before the addition of the new crib that converted into a day bed, the room had a rustic feel. Now the room was filled with items of white for a new life to come--bassinet, rocker, changing table, pampers, car seat, etc. The walls are cedar and the furniture

3

oak. The tree rings visible in the wood paneling and the furniture reflected life. Ean wondered if this is what impressed upon me the desire to bring more life into our home. We argued about the material the crib was made of, and came to the agreement that it would be made of wood, but there was no agreement on the finish. Ean wanted to stay traditional and go with the wood theme but I was not having it.

"It's a boy," said Ean.

"That is why white is better, it is made up of all visible colors."

"Wood is more natural and neutral. Why does everything have to be white?" asked Ean.

"We went over this already."

"I thought we were doing this together."

"We are."

"Since it has been discussed, your decision is final," said Ean.

"It is our discussion," I said.

"But your decision!"

I disputed Ean, did not give in, and won. So there it stood, a bright white lacquer crib. Arguing the child's sex did not seem to sway me. Ean wondered what would happen when we had to name the child. When we argued, I could have won that also but I thought I would let him have it. Tur was his idea. It's rut spelled backwards.

I could see Ean looking up out of the corner of his eye at the stuffed moose head mounted to the far left wall with the engraved label below that read *l'orignal*. Keeping it was another argument he lost. I did not want to get rid of it. In today's market the estimated value of such an item was over two thousand dollars. The taxidermist's dream was left behind by the previous owners along with some books about moose and a warning pamphlet about how more moose were making their way to the North Country of New York State. The previous owners were moose lovers.

When we first moved into the camp I spent some evenings reading the books they had left behind. The moose, I learned, were an interesting species and the largest land mammal in North America. When I tried explaining these facts one night to Ean while we laid in bed, he was not interested.

"They can weigh up to 1200 pounds and can grow up to 6 feet tall. The rut, as the breeding season came to be known, starts in late September, early October."

Ean listened quietly as I told him that male bulls engaged in aggressive displays to gain a mate during the rut and could breed with up to six female cows during this time.

"Sounds to me like the stereotypical gay guy during the hot summer months," said Ean.

"It says here that during the rut the male bull does not eat much, but feeds heavily when it's over to prepare for the upcoming winter. New calves are born in late May and early June. Females go through gestation for 230 days."

"I think I have a name for the baby we'll adopt?"

"And what would that be?"

"We can name him Tur."

"Where did you get that name?"

"Its rut spelled backwards!"

We argued over the name until I let him win, so that I could continue telling him about moose.

"OK, we can name him Tur."

Ean smiled and turned over and leaned to face me as he listened.

"Moose are found in the northeastern U.S., including the Adirondack Mountains."

"We drive through the mountains each weekend when we come up here," said Ean.

"Another interesting fact is that they are strict vegetarians and consume up to 60 pounds of vegetation each day. Their favorite plants include the willow and maple trees. New York does not house any predators of the moose, and its most common threat outside of New York is the grey wolf. Here their most common threat is diseases and ticks."

"That's probably why the population is increasing."

I pulled out the pamphlet left behind that I was using as a book mark and held it up to Ean.

"It says in here that there are approximately 300-500 moose in the state and still growing."

Ean fell asleep that evening as I was telling him more facts about the moose.

"Here you go," I now said as I came up behind him.

Ean stood in the doorway of the guest room converted to a nursery and stared at the crib. I handed him a cup of coffee as I held my cup in the other hand.

I looked at the crib then at Ean and smiled.

"We have to get going," said Ean as he sipped some coffee.

"I know. This is going to be great."

"Our life is going to change."

"It doesn't have to."

"This was such a short weekend, and they will feel even shorter," said Ean as he turned around and left the doorway to the kitchen.

"I thought you wanted this."

"Not as much as you."

"It's not too late to change our minds," I said.

Ean did not respond to my comment because he knew his response would just result in the same outcome as our discussion about the crib. A disagreement would take place but it was my final word that would determine the outcome of the situation, because he always gave in. Deep down I knew that most of my love would be transferred to the baby. I would continue to provide a loving home as we did for each other. I hate to admit it but sometimes I feel like Ean is my child.

I followed behind Ean into the kitchen and walked up behind him as he stood in front of the sink washing his coffee cup. Reaching around his waist I placed my cup in the sink. He grabbed it and rinsed the cup out, then placed it into the dish rack. Ean turned around in my arms and faced me. His almond shaped brown eyes looked at me in dissatisfaction then shut as he leaned into my cheek with his lips and gently kissed me.

"Were going to be late," said Ean.

"Ready when you are."

"Everything is locked up," said Ean as we both headed into the bedroom to grab our bags.

Ean put his backpack on his shoulders as I grabbed my laptop case and headed for the front door.

"Forgetting something?"

"Oh yeah, I almost forgot," I said as I turned around and went into the nursery and retrieved the infant car seat then headed out to the car.

There she was. When I purchased her I thought that was the only baby I was going to need. She looked too pretty in the driveway. My chili red *Mini Cooper* convertible stood firm in her bulldog stance. I loved the white roof and mirror contrast. This baby had a 16 valve alloy engine, all season traction and stability control. Ean thought we should have gotten a mini van with the baby and all but I sold him on the collision protection with the 6 air-bags with air curtain system. I was sold on the multifunction steering wheel system with cruise control and the black leather interior.

As I placed the car seat in the back of the car, Ean locked the front door of the house and jetted to the car so that we could get on the road to Albany where our jobs were waiting for us as they did every Monday morning. There I sat in the driver's seat as Ean my co-pilot sat beside me. The empty car seat laid dead center on the back seat. Ean's mouth was void of words; clearly he processed our morning discussion over coffee. One might think that the ingestion of caffeine in the morning would lift ones spirits and make a person livelier, but in Ean's case it strengthened his mood regardless of whatever mood he was in. Ean eventually leveled out and broke his silence when the car slowed down behind a traffic jam as we rode south on Interstate-87.

"Wonder what's holding us up?"

I hesitated to respond but then decided not to censor myself.

"It's like the adoption process," I said hoping he would get the cue and share with me his reservations about what we were both about to do that week, before it was too late.

"It almost reached the point of an ordeal rather than a process."

"Would you rather not do this?" I asked.

"I want this. It is just that I thought if we raised a child it would be one of our own."

"I'm not about to father a child."

"I wanted the child to truly be ours."

"The child will be ours once it is adopted," I said.

"The process is not natural. It was like shopping," said Ean.

"I know how much you hate shopping."

"We've already picked out our purchase so we might as well take him home."

"I'm glad you're with me on this one."

"This is not how I wanted to go about it."

"Don't worry, my parents will help out."

"Your parents don't even approve of me. What makes you think they will accept the baby?" asked Ean.

"Yes they do."

"You mean they tolerate me."

"I wonder how they will take to the baby knowing they have no biological link or true responsibility," I said.

Ean did not have all the truth of the matter. I once again hesitated and debated with myself whether I should continue this conversation as we stood still in traffic. The morning seemed to get off on a negative start. How could I turn things around? I wanted to turn the car around and head back to our home away from home. Instead, I turned the radio dial to try and get a news station for the latest information on traffic and weather. There were no news stations in these parts, like 1010 WINS or 880 WCBS in New York City. The news report segment that came on did not tell of any traffic problems on Interstate-87 so I turned off the radio. The traffic continued to move at a snail's pace. The congestion was mostly from people trying to get to the Plattsburgh area. As we proceeded south, blue and red flashing lights could be seen up ahead in the distance as the road inclined. A police vehicle with flashing lights drove past us along the shoulder of the road. Little by little the speed of traffic increased as I was able to push down on the accelerator. Ean once again broke his silence.

"It looks like an accident up ahead."

"Hope no one was hurt."

Ean reached into his pocket and pulled out a tin box of *Altoids* and popped one in his mouth. It is a nervous habit of his. Once he started he could chew one after the other until his stomach felt warm.

"Want one?"

"No thanks. Why are you always taking in those empty calories? Those things are full of sugar."

"They are better than *Lifesavers*."

"That will be the day when one of those saves your life," I said.

The car sped up then stopped in a cyclical fashion. Each car is stopped at the scene until it was allowed to pass. As Ean and I drew near we could see what appeared to be the root of the traffic jam. After the wait it turned out not to be an accident but the rescue of l'orignal. One by one the cars stopped to gaze at the sight of the local State Trooper whose car was parked blocking the right lane. The trooper placed flares and bright orange cones a few feet leading up to the scene to direct traffic away toward the left lane. In addition to the police car there was a large vehicle that displayed the name Department of Environmental Conservation (DEC). As we approached the scene, we were stopped. There we could see l'orignal surrounded by men in uniform. He is a large moose measuring six and a half feet tall and weighing 1,450 pounds. His brown coat shined and matched the color of Ean's eyes. By the time we reached him, the DEC had tranquilized him and cut his antlers from the trees and brush in which he had become entangled. L'orignal's large body laid partially on the ground as his head and antlers that span ten feet wide were mangled and dangling from a tree. Ean rolled down the window as we approached Trooper Brian Flannery. Trooper Flannery stood tall with authority in his finely fitting light grey uniform. He moved over to our vehicle and leaned in to the window. His blue eyes sparkled out of his fair complexion covered by a head of gelled back black hair as dark as coal.

"Is it alright?" asked Ean.

"He's fine. Breeding season you know," said Brian.

"Are you sure they're not hurting it?"

"Not at all, they had to cut the antlers to release him. It has to be done a certain way for future identification. They eventually fall off," said Brian as he motioned to Mark Sands of the DEC who placed a GPS device around the moose's neck.

Mark was a tall and rugged looking outdoorsman. He had light brown hair that he pushed out of his face as he reached around the moose's neck to attach the GPS.

"Oh," I said as Ean looked at Mark then back at the Trooper.

"They're not seen very often in these parts, but the population is growing," said Brian as he motioned us to move along.

"See that is what happens when man interferes with nature," said Ean as Brian listened to his words as Ean rolled up the window.

"What do you mean?" I asked as I moved the car forward through the cones.

"If this road wasn't here that moose would probably have been taking a casual stroll through the woods and been able to anticipate it's surroundings. It looked like they had to tranquilize it to keep it down."

"Yeah, you can't keep a good moose down," I said as Ean let out a laugh.

I steered the car through the cones and stepped on the gas to make up the time we lost so that Ean and I would not be late for work. Four hours later I drove up to the front of Ean's office building to drop him off.

"I'll see you at the agency at 5:30," I said as Ean leaned towards me and pursed his lips in my direction. I kissed him.

"Don't forget to bring the car seat," said Ean as he lifted himself out of the car and headed into the office building.

"Love you," Ean shouted to me.

"I love you too."

Ean could not hear my words but he already knew how I feel about him.

~ ~ ~ ~

When I arrived at work that morning, arraignments were waiting for me. There were about fifteen new arrests over the weekend, in addition to the cases that were adjourned to today from two weeks ago. After I checked my e-mail and phone messages I grabbed my pile of files and headed into Courtroom One. All new arrests were arraigned in this courtroom. Being an Assistant District Attorney (ADA) for three years now, I had been hoping to move up to chief ADA. During the three years I have been in this office, I have seen attorneys come and go. The turn over is high with the average length being one and a half years. When I went into the courtroom, Lavonda was already there. Lavonda is a well respected Special Prosecutor who graduated from Columbia Law with honors and headed the law review. She is a tall and thin African-American woman with short cropped hair worn in an afro and dresses impeccably. She always wears finely tailored suites in fabrics and colors appropriate for the season. Lavonda is not only a colleague, but our friend and attorney.

"Tonight is our final class before we bring Tur home," I said.

"All the paperwork for the adoption should be finalized. I submitted it to Jeanine Friday afternoon," said Lavonda.

"Ean set the date for the homecoming for next Friday, you'll be there?"

"I'm preparing for the divorce, but I'll be there."

"How's Ean?"

"He told me the mother was referred to him at his agency."

"It's a small world."

"I think he is having reservations, but he's alright now."

"It's a big commitment," said Lavonda as the court officers opened the courtroom and a large influx of people entered and filled the gallery.

The Judge entered the courtroom and took the bench. After arraignments were completed I let my intern take over and headed back to the office. I left my Blackberry on so he could text me if he had any questions. I went straight to my desk to check email. There was a message from Ean that read:

*Stacy:*

*Sorry about my attitude this morning. I'll see you at the agency tonight.*

*Love Ean.*

As I read the message Ean sat at his desk and put together a referral package for the new client that was assigned to him. He stopped shuffling through the referral package and looked at the phone. He had just sent the email message and wanted to call. Claudia Braunstein is a new mother who just gave birth, and is a second time felon whose charges were reduced from criminal possession of a control substance and a weapon to a misdemeanor possession charge. She is the adopted daughter of a well to do Jewish family from New Haven, Connecticut, caught in the Albany area trying to score a drug supply. She is not a predicate felon since it was only her second felony arrest, so the judge had released Claudia under the supervision of probation and gave her a conditional discharge to the Treatment Alternatives to Street Crime (TASC) mandated substance abuse treatment program. Ean normally handled the mentally ill chemical abusers (MICA) clients; however, there had been a high volume of substance abusers in the criminal justice system and he was assigned the overflow. Ean does not mind because this situation helped him learn about the family background for the task he is about to embark on. Between me, Ean and Lavonda, we all had first hand knowledge of the family history and dynamics of little Tur who would be in our care a week from now. As Ean sealed the referral for Tur's biological mother, his co-worker Saudi, a short Dominican woman, walked over to his desk.

"So Mr. Ean did the baby come home yet?"

"Not yet, we are going to the agency tonight for our final class."

"I am happy for you guys. I think it is a really good thing that you are doing. After discussing that case in team, the baby really needs a good home."

"I left an invitation in your box."

"You should have had a baby shower."

"This is like a shower."

"Let me get back to work. I have four referral packages for clients I'm trying to place," said Saudi.

"It's so frustrating, after all the work 95% of them self-sabotage."

"Most criminal offenders take a plea to a program just so they can get out of jail. The average recidivist time is two months," said Saudi.

"Two months, then the process starts all over," said Ean as Saudi walked away.

~ ~ ~ ~

Later that evening Ean met me at the adoption agency for our final class. The training room of the nursery was a room of peace with soft pastels, blues, pinks and yellows brushed along the walls. The room had four nursing stations equipped with all the necessities of child care. During the previous class our instructor Ruth appeared to be hard on me and she had reason to be. From the first lesson that introduced us both to a plastic model of an infant we were to get acquainted and comfortable with, I appeared clumsy with the child. Ean was a natural. He had exposure and experience growing up in a family with thirteen children. He learned to model his mother and older sister as they cared for and nurtured his siblings.

"No, no," said Ruth in a heavy accent.

Ruth was a four foot three dark West Indian woman with a perm. Her hair was pulled back tight in a knot she calls "one". She dressed in a nurse's uniform with baby bottles and rattles all over.

"Should I hold the baby's head close to my chest?" I asked.

"Yes child, let the baby hear the rhythm of your heart," said Ruth.

"Like this?" I asked and held the plastic doll's head to my chest.

"You got it," said Ruth.

"Yeah, you got it," said Ean as he tried to reassure me.

"As you relax, your heart rate will slow down calming the child," said Ruth in a matter of fact tone.

Ean smiled at my clumsiness and reached up to the doll and adjusted its head closer to my heart.

"You will do fine," said Ruth as she smiled at Ean then me.

Her comment made me feel less of a parent. I was jealous of Ean. His upbringing was so different than mine. My parents, Rona and Aton, were extremely conservative Republicans who were influenced by the idea of a nuclear family and only had two point five children. Having an older sister did not give me the chance to learn about child care. I did however learn from watching my mother care for her Yorkshire terrier. My Jewish mother would fill Misty's bowl with kibbles and water, cuddle her on the sofa, change her outfits for the season and brush and place pink bows in her fluffy hair as my father was at his predominantly Jewish law firm. As I grew older I learned how to play dress up and have tea with my older sister. When she played with her dolls she treated them like adults having adult conversations. I could see myself talking to Ean the way she spoke with her dolls, the same way our mother spoke to us. Today Earl Grey tea is still a favorite of mine, but it won't help me take care of an infant. As I said before, I sometimes feel like Ean is my child, but he is self sufficient. I don't have to change any diapers or burp him. He can be asked whether or not he would like lemon with his tea. Ean can obviously feed himself and change his clothes, though on occasion, I have to instruct him to change soiled clothing. Bathing is also an exception because I sometime scrub his back when we shower together. That is the extent of my child care and rearing experience.

This final class was our true test. We were learning with a real human infant. In ending our lesson I put the baby in the crib on his side and placed his bottle in his mouth. I tucked his pale blue blanket between his soft pajama and mattress for a final practice. This little baby was the ideal child. He was so content that I could only hear his soft breaths being inhaled and soft cooing as he exhaled. The next time I would be tucking a baby in, it will be at home. After tucking the baby in, both Ean and Ruth gave me one last inspection.

"Very good boys," said Ruth as she smiled at us.

"Thank you," said Ean as he retrieved our belongings to head home.

We were about to leave the nursery when Jeanine Morton entered the training room and approached us. Jeanine was the director of the adoption program. She appeared frumpy with scraggly brown hair and a mismatched outfit of green pencil plaid skirt and charcoal sweatshirt. She was a very severe woman.

"I'm glad you're still here," she said.

"Hi," said Ean.

"I need to talk to you both about the adoption. Please come to my office," said Jeanine as both Ean and I looked at one another.

"Sure," I said as we followed Jeanine out of the room waiving goodbye to Ruth as we left.

As we walked down the agency corridors, all were silent. The crisp white walls of the corridor contrasted with the training room. When we reached Jeanine's office she let us in.

"Please take a seat," said Jeanine.

Ean had a concerned look on his face and stared at me as Jeanne got right into it without preparation.

"There is a problem with the adoption," said Jeanine.

"What problem?"

"Because of your relationship…"

"Because we're gay?"

"No, excuse me, I mean because of the length of your relationship we need you to be foster parents first."

"We've been married for three years and have a Canadian marriage license that is now fully recognized in New York State."

"I have your file," said Jeanine.

"What about the classes? I thought they were sufficient," said Ean.

"They are. However, the agency is not willing to sign over full custody of the child unless we are ensured that it will be a perfect match," said Jeanine.

"Ean, and I are a perfect match for Tur," I said.

"We are requiring that you go through a foster period before full custody is awarded," said Jeanine.

"How long will this take?" I asked.

"Possibly a year, maybe longer," said Jeanine.

"You will be hearing from our attorney," I said as I got up to leave.

Ean stayed seated looking up at me.

"When can we take Tur home?" asked Ean.

"You are still scheduled to take him by the end of next week, we just need to finalize the foster care arrangement," said Jeanine.

"We understand," said Ean as I stood and headed for the door, waiting for him to join me in my exodus.

"As stated, you will be hearing from our attorney," I said as Ean got up to join me.

"Good then, we will need the papers signed as soon as possible if you wish to have the child by the end of next week," said Jeanine as Ean and I left her office.

# Chapter II

## Tur

Three days later Lavonda, Ean and I were getting prepared for our day in court. I called Lavonda from my cell phone soon after we leave Jeanine's office. I was furious.

"She has some nerve leading us to believe we would be able to adopt Tur then come to find out we have to be foster parents first."

Ean and I sat in our living room anxiously awaiting Lavonda's arrival.

"Every time I think of our last conversation with Jeanine it infuriates me."

"Calm down, at this point there is nothing we can do," said Ean.

"Let us wait for Lavonda's opinion."

Although I am an attorney and have a good understanding of the law, Ean's comment forced me to face the fact of the situation. The door bell rang. I jumped up from the couch to answer it. I opened the door. Lavonda did not wait for her invitation to come in. She headed for me with a file folder under her arm and kissed me hello then walked right into the apartment without saying a word. I know Lavonda. I had seen her conference many cases and handle a courtroom. Whenever she was presented with a tough situation, little is said on her part. I closed the door and followed her into the living room as Ean stood up to welcome her. She hugged Ean as if she was greeting him at a funeral. Yeah, it is more than just a greeting; she was preparing him for some devastating news.

"Would you like something to drink?" asked Ean.

"No thank you. Let's get to this," said Lavonda.

"Is it legal for them to make us go through a foster care arrangement?" asked Ean.

We all sat down before Lavonda responded.

"I met with Jeanine and they do have every right to guarantee an appropriate placement for the court," said Lavonda.

"These were not the terms of our arrangement," I said.

"There is nothing in writing. Besides you will have legal guardianship until the full adoption is granted," said Lavonda.

I loved Lavonda. She always had a way of delivering good news with the bad. I've heard her deliver news to many defense attorneys regarding plea offers the District Attorney's office was willing to put on the table.

"How long is that going to take?" I asked.

"Not long. The mother is fully on board and Jeanine and the agency are fully cooperating. The mother is fully aware of who you both are and agrees with the placement. I have been running around all morning for the signatures."

"What about the father?" asked Ean.

"Artificial Insemination," said Lavonda.

"Do you mean a sperm donor?" asked Ean.

"Who ever he is, he gave up his rights."

Lavonda looked at me then continued.

"All parties except you two have signed off. I just need your signatures so that we can have the paperwork ready for the judge on Friday."

She took the file folder which was sitting on her lap and handed it to me. I snatched it from her hand and opened the folder to review the papers.

"When a male donates his sperm rights are not automatically forfeited."

"Stacy," said Ean.

I glanced up at him not liking it when he challenged me.

"This is a life we are all talking about," said Ean.

"And," I said.

"Well, it is not the same as haggling with a dealership for a new vehicle. Remember when you purchased the *Mini Cooper*?" asked Ean.

"What about it?" I asked.

"This is different. We are talking about a human life," said Ean.

"Already established," I said.

Ean annoyed me when he repeats himself. Lavonda sat silently as she watched the both of us go back and forth. She never saw us argue. What got to me was that Ean was right. Lavonda was here, so I thought I would give him another win.

"You're right," I said.

Lavonda looked at Ean and smiled. As I observed her, she had done the same to me while before the bench. She knew I didn't like to lose an argument. There was no judge or jury and Ean was right.

"The papers are in top shape, they just need your signature," said Lavonda as she pulled a pen out of her jacket pocket and passed it to me. I signed and dated the last two pages and handed the file to Ean.

"Where do I sign?" asked Ean.

Ean was nervous whenever he had to sign official legal documents. He had the same expression on his face when we signed the papers at the closing for our camp up north in the town of Mooers.

"The last two pages by the red X. Jeanine will send over a representative tomorrow after work for your fingerprints and to look at the apartment. They will also be sending you a startup check for supplies, you know, diapers, formula," said Lavonda.

Ean signed the papers and handed the file folder back to Lavonda.

"I'll have copies for you on Friday. I really have to get going," said Lavonda as she got up from the sofa.

"I'll see you on Friday?" I asked.

"Family Court 10:00 a.m. sharp. Since all parties are on board with the arrangement I don't see why the judge would disagree. Our appearance should be just a formality. The agency will transfer custody to you then," said Lavonda.

Those words comforted me. Ean smiled nervously at Lavonda as she headed for the door.

"See you then," I said as she unlocked the apartment door and left.

"This is really going to happen," said Ean.

"Yeah, are you OK with it?" I asked and put my arm around him.

"Yes," said Ean, but still sounded a bit unsure of himself.

"What do you want to do today? We have the whole day to ourselves," I said.

"Actually, I thought I would go visit my sister today."

"Alright, we'll have tonight together," I said as Ean went to the closet door and retrieved his jacket.

"Can I take the *Mini*?"

"Be gentle with her."

"I'll see you later today," said Ean as he put his jacket on, grabbed the car keys off the table and left the apartment.

~ ~ ~ ~

Ean drove into the driveway of his sister's colonial home. It is a huge house for just two people. Erica and Leo occupied the home. Erica spends most of her time in half of the second floor which was converted to an artist studio. The studio is a place where Erica had her artist friends over to create their next masterpieces. Erica is Ean's older sister. The two of them are inseparable. They share the kind of bond that most people say is found only among twins. Erica is a female version of Ean; however, she is shorter and a little bit rounder. She has Ean's complexion and dark hair. Her eyes are similar to his but lighter. She is a trained artist, a S.U.N.Y Purchase graduate. She stays home all day while her husband, Leo, is away at work. Leo immigrated to the United States in the late eighties after the fall of communism when the Berlin wall came crashing down, the glory days of the Reagan administration. He is good with numbers, a financial analyst for the controller's office.

Ean walked up to the door and rang the bell. After about two minutes Erica answered the door dressed in a blue cotton bathrobe. Her hair was still wet from a shower. She ran a large black comb through her hair.

"Hi, sweetie," she said as she kissed her brother.

Ean walked into the foyer of the home and began climbing the stair to the second floor studio. Erica followed behind him. As Ean entered the studio he peeled off his jacket and took a seat on one of twelve stools that stood around an oversized drafting table.

"It's really getting cold," said Erica.

"You think this is cold you should come to the North Country more often. We haven't even had our first snow."

"It will be soon enough. How's the hubby?"

"He's ecstatic. We ran into a glitch with the adoption but it was all straightened out this morning. Lavonda was over and we signed the official papers to be the child's foster parents."

"Foster parents? I thought you were adopting."

"We are, but they are having us be foster parents first with full guardianship."

"Is everything alright? You don't sound so enthusiastic."

"I am. It's just that he pushed for this and he really didn't think about what I fully wanted. It's not the ideal situation for me. Everything seemed fine until I had to sign on the dotted line this morning."

"It is a little late to be unsure. You're scheduled to bring the baby home on Friday. I made arrangements and ordered party favors," said Erica.

"Yeah, and I told my supervisor that I needed to cut my hours at work. They are not expecting me to resign," said Ean.

"Why do you have to resign?"

"Stacy wants me to, but I have to contribute. I don't want to be 100% dependent on him."

"It's not so bad."

Ean did not want Erica's arrangement.

"When I evaluate my relationship now, it looks like the relationship of someone in a domestic violence situation," said Ean.

"Come on! What's really going on?" asks Erica, knowing her brother was camouflaging his true concerns.

"I don't know if I can do this alone."

"What about your husband?"

"He will be at work all day and I know I will be mostly responsible for the baby. I'm stressed because now I am going to have to be responsible for something. For example, when we purchased the house up north, Stacy became responsible for keeping it clean, dusting, mopping, and mowing the grass during the summer months, putting up and taking down the storm windows in the winter months, not to mention the daily functions of living like cooking, washing dishes and clothes, shopping. This will all be heavily compounded by the new addition and will default to me," said Ean.

"Sounds like some control issues going on. Maybe you should talk to him."

"We tried to have this discussion but it always ends up his way. When I wanted a baby I wanted to have my own."

"What did he say?"

"It's difficult to get him to see things my way. I know that I'm gay and the average woman probably would not want to have a child with a gay man. But I wanted a child of my own."

"Friday you will have a child of your own. What are you going to do about this?" asked Erica.

"That is why I am here. I really need your help with this."

"What do you need me to do?"

"I'm only scheduled to work three days out of the week. Can you help babysit Tuesday through Thursday?"

Erica looked at her pile of empty ecru canvasses piled against the wall then glanced at her new set of acrylics Leo has just surprised her with and smiled at Ean.

"Sure," said Erica.

"I will pay you for your help."

Erica was quite relaxed until Ean mentioned a fee for service arrangement. She did not like the idea of having a job.

"No, that is quite alright, besides he will be my nephew."

"Are you sure?"

"Quite sure," said Erica as Ean got up from the stool and hugged his sister.

"I owe you."

"We will have the baby this Friday and my new hours start next week. Can you meet us in court? We can let Lavonda know that you will be helping to take care of the baby."

"I can be there. What time?"

"Ten, at the Family Courthouse."

"Hey, there is a new French Café that just opened next door to the Family Court. Do you want to have lunch?" asked Erica.

"Do they serve crepes?"

"They serve a variety of them. They had a good review in the *Times Union* this past weekend. Let me get dressed."

"We can talk about the baby's homecoming party. I already gave out invitations for Friday."

"Don't worry, everything will be ready," said Erica as she left the drafting table and walked through a door that lead to her bedroom.

Ean called to tell me that he was going to be home later than planned.

~ ~ ~ ~

My cell phone rang as I stood in the lobby of the Family Court building. I recognized it was Ean by the type of ring that chimed from my phone. I programmed each number with distinguishing ring tones so that I will know who was calling.

"Where are you?"

"We're on our way," said Ean.

"What's taking you so long?"

"Erica has been trying to contact the caterer all morning."

"We have to be in the courtroom in ten minutes."

Lavonda looked at her watch.

"We're about that much time away. See you soon."

I turned to Lavonda.

"They're on their way."

"I want us to enter all together to make a good impression on the judge. You know, a family unit," said Lavonda.

She knew best. This was her forum and she knew all the players, judges, clerks and law guardians. As Lavonda and I stood there in walked Jeanine followed by Ruth pushing a stroller and another suited male employee. As they passed by Lavonda got their attention.

"Jeanine!"

Jeanine turned her head around towards us. Ruth also looked over and recognized me. The four of them approached. Lavonda was trying to buy time in hopes that Ean would get there soon. She thought it will look best if we all walk in together.

"Shall we go in?" asked Jeanine.

Lavonda nodded her head and began to walk toward courtroom three. As we approached the courtroom door Ean and Erica came dashing through the metal detectors and sprinted to catch up with us. We all headed into the court as a family unit looking good with the additional support of the agency. Judge Lamb was already sitting on the bench. Both parties divided like the Red sea once before the court. Lavonda went up to the court clerk.

"We're number six on the docket. All parties are present and ready to go forward."

The clerk just looked at her and smiled. Judge Lamb was finalizing a support petition for the case before him and the attorney for the petitioner made one last request.

"Your honor, we recommend that the order of protection currently in place be modified to a no illegal contact order at the petitioner's request for unrestricted contact."

The judge granted the modification for no illegal contact and attorneys for both parties shook hands with the law guardian and left the courtroom. The clerk pulled our file from a group of files on her desk and passed it to the judge who announced the matter for the record as Lavonda, Jeanine and the agency's attorney approached the bench. All three discussed the case for thirty minutes before Judge Lamb granted the custody order and instructed Jeanine, as representative of the agency, to hand over the child to its new guardian. Jeanine motioned to Ruth who got up from her seat and pushed the carriage in our direction. She stopped before us with a huge smile on her face.

"Congratulations, boys," said Ruth as everyone in the courtroom watched.

Ean, Erica and I got up and I took the stroller from Ruth. The three of us look at Ruth.

"Thank you."

We turned our heads in the Judge's direction.

"Thank you."

Lavonda, Janice and the agency's attorney approached.

"Thank you for everything," I said.

"Take good care of him. Will be in touch soon," said Jeanine as she left the courtroom.

"I'll catch up with you later," said Lavonda as she followed Jeanine out of the room with the agency's attorney.

Ruth stood behind and walked out with us.

"There is formula, diapers and wipes in this bag at the bottom of the stroller. Compliments of the agency," said Ruth.

We said our goodbyes in the lobby of the courthouse and headed for the *Mini*.

"Go ahead I will meet you at the apartment. Congratulations," said Erica as she left.

Ean and I got to the *Mini* and transferred Tur into the car seat. He was all bundled up in blankets to protect him from the cold. After strapping him in and folding the stroller I put the stroller in the back seat and hopped in the car to head home.

"We did it."

"Yeah, we are both the proud parents of a little rut," said Ean.

When Ean and I arrived at the apartment my heart dropped when we walked through the front door. Struck with the vision of his efforts I truly appreciated him. The house is decorated with blue and white streamers and balloons. It was gaudy, resembling my five year-old birthday party my mother Rona had planned for me with Ms. Green my kindergarten teacher. The decorations were complete with a welcome home sign and stuffed animal stork. I carried Tur into the living room and placed him in the bassinet. Both Ean and I remained staring at him as he slept so angelically. As soon as we settled in Ean got on the phone with the caterer. Apparently they had the wrong day.

"What do you mean?"

"We planned this for the ninth and the person who took the order wrote down the nineteenth," said Ean.

"Are they going to be able to do it?"

"Keep your voice down or you'll wake the baby."

"Well can they do it?"

"Yeah, however, there is a change of plans with the menu. They will only be able to do light fare. They have extras from a function they catered this morning."

"Great, everyone will be expecting a meal," I said.

"We'll just have to explain when they arrive, unless you want to whip something up for thirty people," said Ean.

"Hors d'oeuvres will have to do."

"I thought so," said Ean as the door bell rang.

"I'll get it. It's probably my parents. They always get to a function hours before it begins."

When I opened the door, Erica was standing in the hallway with bags of refreshments. She lifted the bags and handed them to me. I took them into the kitchen as she went into the living room.

"Where is he?" she asked as she walked in.

"Over here," said Ean as he motioned her over to him.

Erica walked over to the Bassinet and examined Tur then turned to Ean and hugged him.

"I'm so proud of you," said Erica.

"Hey, I finally got in touch with the caterers. It's a disaster. I'll fill you in. Let's get the tables ready. We are only going to need napkins," said Ean as he took Erica's hand and lead her into the kitchen.

As Ean and Erica entered the kitchen the phone rang. I picked up the receiver from the phone mounted on the wall.

"Hello."

"Stacy, it's your mother," she said as she took in a deep breath and let it out slowly.

"Are you on your way?"

"Your father and I will not be able to make it today."

"Is everything alright?"

"We're fine, it's just that we're not ready yet to meet the new addition to the family."

"Alright, I'll see you soon," I said and hung up the phone.

"Are they on their way?" asked Ean.

"Not today."

Ean walked over and hugged me.

"We'll we have twenty-eight other people to feed and entertain."

Five hours later everyone else who we invited showed up with gifts. Ean worked the room and introduced his co-worker Saudi to Lavonda and Erica while Artie Shaw's 1940's version of *Stardust* played on the CD player. Everyone took a turn to see Tur when they arrived. After a while we had to limit the time each person spent with him, not only for germs but so that he could rest. We had a long trip up to our camp to spend the first weekend with Tur alone. Ean and I made a brief speech thanking everyone for coming and sharing the special moment in our lives. We also apologized for the short notice we had to give them about the dinner arrangement and told them that we understood if they needed to leave earlier to grab dinner before the night was over. Many of the guests decided to leave early. Their early departure was not only so that they could have a dinner somewhere else, but because we were having some difficulty with Tur. About two hours into the party, Tur began to get restless. He was unable to get to sleep. We moved him into the bedroom where Erica kept an eye on him as Ean and I entertained our guests. After a while a continuous crying that escalated came from the bedroom. Ean went to check on Erica to see if she needed anything.

"Is he alright?"

"I think he is over stimulated. Too much excitement and tired," said Erica as she rocked Tur in her arms.

"Can you warm this bottle?"

Ean took the bottle from her hand and went to the kitchen to run it under hot water. I was in the kitchen talking to Lavonda.

"How is it going?"

"Erica thinks he is over stimulated, too much excitement."

"I'm going to get going," said Lavonda.

"OK. Thank you for everything," said Ean.

"The bill is in the mail."

Both Ean and I laughed knowing that Lavonda agreed to represent us out of friendship and her struggle for the rights of gay couples to adopt the great number of children who need a loving and caring home. As Tur's cries continued to escalate, the other guests approached Ean and I to say goodnight. Ean headed back into the bedroom to give Erica the bottle. She quickly tested the temperature of the milk on the back of her hand then placed it in Tur's mouth. Tur began to suck on the nipple and quieted down. Erica stayed with us that first night and coached us after everyone left. Her instructions were different than Ruth's. Ruth's handling of the child was soft but a bit mechanical. Erica, on the other, hand was delicate throughout her interaction with Tur. She had a softness to her that Ean sometimes expressed with me in his touch. They both possessed a mother's love that is passed on from generation to generation in a matrilineal clan. When the last guests left Ean and I cleaned up the apartment and took over for Erica.

The next morning Ean got up early and made breakfast. Before he left the room he looked into the bassinet to get a glimpse of Tur. The reality still had not settled in. Ean went into the kitchen and made a large stack of French toast with sliced strawberries and bananas sprinkled with confectioner's sugar. I climbed out of bed and peered into the bassinet just as Ean had done. Tur was sound asleep. I stared at his dark pink skin and watched his chest rise and fall as he took short and long breaths. Like Ean, I could not believe I was a foster parent and that the adoption was actually going to happen. I could smell the warm cinnamon that filled the air and headed for the kitchen to wish Ean the first good morning as a family. Before going into the kitchen I stopped and peeked into the living room where Erica laid sound asleep on the sofa. Erica was snoring softly just as Ean sometimes did when he fell asleep next to me. Erica was in our room on both occasions when Tur woke up. She immediately responded to his call and flew into the room before Ean or I could get out of bed. She had a mother's instinct and she proved to be the right person to help take care of our child.

Ean herd me get up and came out into the living room carrying a cup of coffee for me. He whispered, trying not to wake up Erica.

"Here you go, sweetie. Did you sleep alright?"

"Yeah."

"Come on, let her get some rest," said Ean as he held on to my arm and directed me to the kitchen.

We must have woken up Erica because she walked into the kitchen right behind us.

"The food smells good. I should probably get the baby up soon to eat. They have to be put on a schedule."

"You just fed him at two in the morning," I said.

"We saw you come in and out last night," said Ean.

"He finally settled down. Too much excitement," said Erica.

The three of us sat at the table and ate breakfast before Tur started to call.

"Everything is packed for the weekend," said Ean.

"Yeah, I thought we would get an early start. Are you sure you don't want to come with us?" I asked.

"Don't worry, you will have me over soon enough. Besides, I'm your official Au Pair during the week," said Erica.

I wanted to get an early start on the road and get my new family up to the North Country. Ean decided to drive while I took care of Tur. We decided that we would rotate the responsibility by taking turns. With our new family I was going to be the first to care for him. I sat in the back seat of the *Mini* while Ean was driving so that I could attend to Tur if he needed me. With the exception of last night, it seemed as if this was not going to be as difficult as I had imagined it would be. Tur slept most of the ride. Ruth and Erica had explained that newborns slept often and would cry to let a parent know they were hungry, tired, or needed to be changed. Ruth as the baby developed it will begin to want stimulation and attention. This should be easy, I thought to myself. I thought too soon. As Ean and I got further north on Interstate-87, Tur woke and began to cry. I first tried to feed him but he would not take the bottle.

I then checked for a wet diaper but he felt warm
and dry as a desert. As I looked into his eyes, I try
to get his attention to stimulate him but he began
to cry louder.

"Hello, little one. Hello."

This irritated him more. I tried to do
everything I was taught but it just seemed to
frustrate him as the crying got louder. I then tried
to rock him in the car seat but it was bolted in by
the seatbelt.

"He probably has gas."

"Let's pull over at the next rest area."

"It's not for another three miles."

As Ean pulled into the next rest area Tur was
in the back seat screaming bloody murder.

"It must be a gas pain."

Ean got out of the car and into the cold
without his jacket and came around to the
passenger's seat. I quickly opened the door and
hopped out of the car as Ean reached in to
unbuckle the car seat and took Tur into the rest
area. It was cold and began to snow. The rest area
was warm inside and smelled of disinfectant.
There was a truck also parked outside. I followed
behind Ean into the men's room. Ean placed the
car seat on the baby changing station in the men's
room and lifted Tur out of the car seat. He held
him over his shoulder and patted his back as he
gently jerked his body up and down. Tur let out a
large belch and hurled milk over Ean's shoulder.
The baby stopped crying for a moment then began
again but with less force. Ean then checked Tur's
diaper.

"He's wet."

"He didn't feel wet when I checked him."

"When its warm its sometimes hard to detect it."

"Hand me the wipes and a diaper."

"Where are they?"

"I left the bag in the car."

"I'll get it."

I quickly ran out of the men's bathroom to get the bag.

"It's on the back seat!" shouted Ean.

Maybe this was going to be more difficult than I thought. At that moment I got an adrenaline rush. It felt common to the feeling right before I'm about to change a tire when I got a flat on the road. That's what it began to feel like. Ruth went over this with us but it is different when the instructor was gone and you're on your own. Solo.

As Ean changed Tur a toilet flushed and a man dressed in black and red hunters flannel came out of one of the stalls and bypassed the sinks without washing his hands. As he left he glared at Ean and I.

"Where's the baby's mama?"

"You're looking at her," I said.

The man ignored me and kept on walking.

"Queers!" he shouted as he leaves.

I turned away from Ean to go after him so that I can beat the shit out of him but Ean grabbed my arm and held me back.

"Let it go!"

Tur quieted down and Ean prepared him in the car seat to head back to the vehicle. We both got back in the car. The truck that was parked when we got there was gone. Ean and I continued to head north. As soon as Ean accelerated on the road Tur once again began to cry. I try to console him, however, nothing I did worked. It is my turn and I was trying my best to handle and deal with what I had asked for. Rona always told me to be careful what I wished for. The thought of her voice in my head annoyed me especially since she did not bring herself to go against my father and come to see Tur. I know it was his doing.

As Ean drove I tried my best to quiet Tur. Ean was a wreck when he drove and did not like to drive with any noise in the car. He would not turn on the radio and the windows had to be fully closed. In the summer he rolled up the windows and did not put on the air conditioner because of the noise. If Tur was not with us he would not have the heater on in this weather while driving. The *Mini* approached the next exit.

"Do you think we can change places?"

"I'll pull over here on the shoulder."

Tur had quieted as Ean slowed the car down and pulled over.

The car stopped. Tur started to cry again as I opened the door and hopped out. I got up front to take the wheel. It was a good thing Ean truly did not like to drive. As we drove Ean worked his magic. Ean watched Tur all the way to the cottage as he slept the rest of the ride.

# Chapter III

## Collide

This was exhausting. We've only been with Tur for a few months. I sat in the rocker by the crib holding and feeding him. It was my turn. Ean had been good to me all day. We agreed to rotate but he was being kind taking care of Tur's needs. He knew I am easily frustrated and could not deal. We both were exhausted. Ruth had continuously reminded us throughout our trainings that taking care of a child is a great responsibility. Lavonda said having a child was not like having a pet. Her exact words were: "You can't just take it for a walk and throw a bowl of food down and expect it to occupy itself." I held Tur up to my chest as Ruth instructed but I was stressed and I knew Tur was absorbing every uneven beat of my heart. I began take deep breaths to calm my nerves. It was clear why Tur was so colicky. Not only was he taken away from his crack addicted biological mother, but he was ripped from one drug addicted parent and given over to a neurotic one.

As I glanced at the digital clock on the dresser it read 2:30am and Tur finally fell asleep. As I sat there I just stared in my arms at Tur and thought about the life I want to give him. Like most parents I wanted the world for this child. This night I promised not just to give Tur love but to nurture and help him flourish in all aspects of his life. As I held him tightly I lifted myself out of the chair and gently placed him in the crib. Tur's eyes rolled back and forth under his pink eyelids as he sucked on the bottle's nipple as I firmly tucked the blanket below the bottle and near the pillow to hold the bottle in place. My practice with the baby at the agency paid off. I gave Tur a soft kiss on his forehead as I sometimes do Ean. I went over to the desk and pulled out my journal to continue documenting our time with Tur in the cabin and when I was done I slipped the journal back into the drawer, closed it and turned the key. I was too tired to take the key out of the drawer and hide it as I usually did. No, that was too much work. Before I left the room I did, however, effortlessly glance at the baby monitor to ensure it was on before I headed off to bed.

When I entered the bedroom Ean was snoring. I walked over to my side of the bed and lifted myself out of my slippers and slide into the bed beside him and pulled the covers over my shoulders. Ean spooned my body.

"I love you," he said sleepily.

"Love you to," I said and fell asleep.

A few hours later Ean and I awoke to the sounds of Tur's cries coming out of the baby monitor. Since he's been with us, Tur woke up every morning like clock work. It was an hour earlier than we usually rise. Ean opened his eyes and looked at me with great disappointment. It was his turn.

"Why haven't you checked on Tur," he asked as he pushed himself up out of the bed.

Tur's cries got louder as Ean grabbed his robe off the chair by the bed and put it on. It was getting colder by the day and so was Ean. Ean left the room. After a few seconds I shouted out to him.

"Is he alright?"

"He's fine, I think he is just hungry," said Ean through the baby monitor.

Ean came back into the room carrying Tur.

"We have to get ready," said Ean as he held a bottle in Tur's mouth and rocked back and forth.

Tur squirmed in his arms.

"I think he brought a gift into the world. Would you like to change him?"

I turned over and pulled the covers over my head. I was nice and warm. Knowing I had to get up I just wanted to get into a hot shower and in my warm clothing.

"I didn't think so," snapped Ean as he turned around and left to the nursery.

It was his turn. As Ean left the room I climbed out of bed and headed for the bathroom to take a shower.

Ean entered the nursery and placed Tur back in the crib. Tur once again began to cry. Ean undressed Tur and changed his diaper as I showered. After my shower I dressed and went into the nursery. There Ean stood above the crib looking down on Tur. The smell of fresh coffee and baby powder filled the air.

"He should sleep through the ride," said Ean.

"How much of the bottle did he drink?"

"Not much, he just needed to be changed."

"Go get ready, I'll take it from here," I said while Ean frowned.

I grabbed him as he headed out the room and hugged him. He pulled away as I softly kissed his cheek. Ean looked at me sternly.

"Since the baby got home I feel as if I have been doing most of the work, feeding, changing diapers, burping him, you know."

"You're better at this than I am."

"That does not mean you cannot try. You took the same child classes that I did."

"Come on, go get ready," I said as Ean pulled away from me and left the room.

He was right. We disagreed on everything. It always had to be my way. I had to be right and always win an argument. Also when we are in the middle of a disagreement I had to gain control and dismiss everything including his feelings and order him to do something. I'm a master at diversion plays. Feeling the guilt I decided to take some of the responsibility that morning and got Tur ready for our trip back to Albany. I padded the car seat with Tur's plushy blue blanket and pillow then lifted him out of the crib and placed him in it. As Tur slept and Ean showered I got all the bags ready and prepared the cooler for the baby's bottles.

Ean dressed then went into the kitchen to drink a half cup of coffee. He returned to the nursery.

"Everything is ready, I said.

Ean took one final run through the house to make sure the house was in order for our return next weekend. Ean reached for the car seat and carried Tur out into the driveway as I grabbed the bags. As Ean securely strapped Tur in the back seat of the car I placed the bags in the trunk of the car. I shut the trunk and went around to the passenger's side of the car to hug Ean. As I wrapped my arms around him I whispered in his ear.

"Life is good," I said.

"Yeah, it is. We better get going. Erica is waiting for us."

There was such a burden lifted off our shoulders when she agreed to take care of Tur while we worked. These days it is so difficult finding child care. It was especially difficult when explaining our foster arrangement that both Ean and I were both going to be working parents. The agency frowns on the fact that we would be having someone else care for Tur while we were out of the house. I think it went over well that it was Ean's sister who would be parenting the child during the day. The fact that the child would have a female caretaker in its presence was also a plus. Ean and I both got into the car and drove off to first drop Tur off with Erica then off to work.

As we drove down Interstate-87 I glanced back into the rear view mirror to get a glimpse of Tur. Ean was right, Tur was going to sleep comfortably through the ride. Both Ean and I were silent and calmed by the sounds of Tur's breath as he inhaled and exhaled. It was mesmerizing and simultaneously soothing as it put me in a trance-like state. It didn't help that I just got a minimal amount of sleep the night before. I still wanted to sleep. It was still dark out and the sun was on its way up to illuminate the sky. I put on the headlights and pressed on the gas to 70 mph and hit the cruise control button on my multifunctional steering wheel to rest my driving leg. Ean and I turned to look at one another and I smiled then faced forward. Life is good, I thought to myself. Ean continued to look at me with his tender eyes. I turned once again to look at him. As I turned to him I reach up with my right hand to put on the overhead light. Ean's pupils shrank in response to the light then quickly enlarged with his eye lids as he quickly turned his head and let out a scream. It was too late.

It happened so quickly. There went *l'orignal.* The car hit the lower part of the moose's huge body as his upper body part went flying across the hood of the car and crashed through the windshield. Ean saw him prior to the hit and quickly prepared his body for impact. My response, however, was delayed. All six airbags inflated; however, the upper back of the moose shattered the windshield and crushed the side column of the car that kept the windshield in place on the driver's side. L'orignal's antlers that were carved for identification were so sharp at the tips that they punctured my air-bag as he crushed the steering wheel. I could not see the road or turn the wheel of the car. The car flew in the direction of the guard rail and spun around when I firmly pressed my right foot onto the brake. The last thing I heard after the glass shattering was Tur cries from the back seat. L'orignal's body bounced off the side of the car and hit the ground. The horn of the car continued to blow as the steering wheel stood crushed into my lap. L'orignal lifted himself off the ground and limped off the side of the road and into the forest.

There was a snapping in my ears. The sound was not from l'orignal making his way through the forest brush but the base of my spine at the back of my neck. I could not feel any pain, nor could I feel my body. There were still sounds around me.

"Stacy... Stacy!" I heard Ean's sweet voice calling.

Tur's cries were also heard between his calls. I could not respond. My throat felt like someone was standing on it.

Three minutes later a woman approached our car.

"Don't move I'll call for an ambulance," said the female voice.

I tried to open my eyes to fight the sleep but could only see a blurred silhouette.

The woman started screaming into a phone.

"There has been an accident on Interstate-87 near exit 34. A car hit a moose. Yes, the Ausable Forks exit for Lake Placid and Saranac Lake, the road marker reads 139 miles. It looks like two males and a baby," said the female voice.

Tur was still crying. Is it my turn? Ean was trying to wake me. It must have been my turn. My name and the sound of Tur's cries were the last sounds I heard before I drifted into a deep sleep.

Thirty minutes later Trooper Flannery arrived with two ambulances, a fire truck and Mark of the DEC. When Brian approached the vehicle the woman who called them ran up to him and pulled him in the direction of the back of the car and pointed out Tur. The doors on the passengers' side of the car were not damaged. Brian motioned to the paramedics. The paramedics opened the back door on Ean's side of the car and quickly removed Tur from the back seat. Tur was no longer crying. They put him in the first ambulance. Brian stood on the passenger's side of the car and opened the front door and tried to talk to Ean.

"Stay still. Do not move."

Ean did not respond. The sun rose in the distance. Brian pulled a small flashlight off his belt and flashed it in Ean's face. Ean blinked.

"Can you hear me?"

Brian flashed the light on Ean's hands that were lacerated and covered with glass.

"Yes."

His response was monotone. His reflexes curled him up in a ball on the seat and shielded him from the blow of the moose's impact. Ean was obviously in shock. He did not move. A paramedic reached in with a neck brace and snapped it around his neck.

"Can you move?" asked the paramedic.

"Yes."

As they helped Ean out of the vehicle and placed him on a lift board the fire department was busy ripping open the door on my side of the car to get at me.

I was not so lucky. My face was covered in blood and glass was imbedded in my skin. I did not feel any pain because I loss all sensation in my body. The fireman removed the door then worked on getting the steering wheel from my lap. Once that was peeled back I was cautiously removed and placed into the second ambulance. A news van from WPTX channel 5 arrived and parked along the yellow marking tape. Ling Han was the news station's token Asian reporter. She hopped out of the vehicle and approached the accident carrying her microphone. Brian saw Ling approaching and quickly left Ean to get control over the scene. He darted in Ling's direction raising his arms ordering her and her cameraman to stay behind the yellow tape.

"I'm willing to give you the story, I just ask that you cooperate," said Brian.

"Ling Han Channel 5 news," said Ling as she looked at Brian's name tag.

"I know," said Brian.

"Mr. Flannery, we want to go live with this exclusive," said Ling.

"Just a moment," said Brian.

As he waived the last ambulance off, the camera man quickly popped off his lens and began taping the scene. The cameraman was able to catch the ambulance departure on tape. The ambulance driver noticed the cameraman as he drives off and put on the siren and flashing lights. As the three of us were transported to Champlain Valley Physicians Hospital (CVPH) Brian stayed behind to clear up the highway. The scene of the accident was coned and taped off. Mark of the

DEC was cleared to track the moose. He walked off to the side of the road and looked for moose tracks. *L'orignal* was long gone but left his hoof prints behind. As Mark stepped off the road and into the grass he saw a small black square object that looked familiar. He looked back at Brian.

"Oh, shit," said Mark as he lifted his left leg.

Brian smiled at Mark.

"Literally," said Brian.

"Literally," said Mark as he wiped his boot along a grassy knoll as he continued to walk onto the grass and bent down to pick up the object.

He held up the object to Brian.

"He went in this direction," shouted Mark as Brian walked toward Mark circling around the dung.

"What's that?" asked Brian.

"GPS, it looks like we were monitoring this one. It must have detached from the accident," said Mark as he put it in his jacket pocket.

Brian stopped behind Mark who was now crouched down with his left knee in the grass. Brian watched Mark as he pulled out a retractable tape measure to calculate the size of the prints *l'orignal* left behind.

"Eight point five inches," said Mark as he got up to measure the moose's stride.

"What does that tell you?" asked Brian as Mark ignored him and continued his work.

"The stride is 51," said Mark as Brian followed his lead and stood near him as he shouted out figures.

"Inches?" asked Brian.

"I just need to calculate the straddle then take a global look at the trail. So far it is looking like a very mature bull," said Mark as he took the measuring tape and extended it across the opposite direction of the moose's trail.

"That must be one big moose considering the damage it did to that vehicle," said Brian.

"This trail is 14 inches wide," said Mark.

"What is all this telling you?" asked Brian hoping this time Mark would answer the question.

"These measurements are almost identical to the bull we cut out of the tree the last time I saw you," said Mark.

"You think it's the same moose?"

"We're not that far from the last encounter," said Mark as he followed the tracks deeper into the woods then backtracked.

Brian stood still and watched him as he worked.

"This moose is beginning to be a regular."

"The prints are a little off than normal. The points should be to the side, back or above the front foot track; however, it looks like the moose is compensating for its weight. It must definitely be hurting from the accident. The stride of that moose we cut out of the tree was 54 inches, this must be the same moose. Moose are usually sloppy in their train pattern but this one left a trail as if it drank a fifth of *Barcardi*," said Mark.

"This moose is making a nuisance of itself."

"Don't worry. The DEC has remedies for that."

"What do you have in mind?"

"If this is the same moose, well it has two strikes against it. Not only becoming a nuisance but a danger to self and others."

"Suicide assessment," said Brian.

"What we normally do in these situations is relocate the animal to a safer environment," said Mark as they both headed for the road.

"Do you have everything you need?" asked Brian.

"Yeah, it looks like I'm all set."

"We'll be in touch."

"I'll double check the number on the GPS locator and let you know if it is our same moose."

"I'll keep you posted on the family," said Brian as he walked Mark to his vehicle.

A tow truck driver approached Brian for clearance and Brian waived him off. The traffic on the road was at a steady pace with cars slowing down to rubberneck. After the tow truck driver received clearance he cleared the scene of his truck. Brian was the last one left at the scene. He took up the cones and removed some of the tape that was strung along the trees marking the scene. Brian left some of the tapes behind just in case he had to return to the scene of the accident. Once that was all cleared up Brian hopped in his car and headed for the hospital.

~ ~ ~ ~

At the hospital I was wheeled into the emergency room. Ean was lying on a bed as he talked to Dr. Rachelle Braun. Tur was in his car seat beside him. They were fine. When they rolled me in the doctor turned from Ean and headed in my direction. She was the head doctor on call for the emergency unit and they were expecting us. Dr. Braun and the nursing staff surrounded my stretcher as they pushed me into an empty docking station for new arrivals. The paramedic that led me into the room continued to pump oxygen into my lungs. One of the nurses grabbed the pump from the paramedic.

"We'll take it from here," said the nurse.

The paramedic read off his version of the events and diagnosis to the doctor before he left.

"His car hit a moose about an hour ago on I 87. Blunt chest trauma with rib fracture, flailed chest with inspiration. Fractured ribs are moving inward preventing intake of oxygen," said the paramedic.

English translation, Stacy's a mess.

"Thank you," said Dr. Braun as she looked at the paramedics' craftsmanship.

To manage the trauma they worked on me during the ride and provided textbook trauma management for blunt chest trauma. The paramedics fashioned a splint and dressing over the broken ribs bulging out of my chest preventing me from inhaling. A portable x-ray machine was wheeled in and placed over me. The technician put in the film, positions the machine and shouted X-ray! The staff went running for clearance. The nurse who took over the pump from the paramedic pulled the pump out of my mouth and ran. They were like roaches that scatter when you enter a dark room and turn on the light. All were gone in a matter of seconds and returned when it was over.

"We need to check for myocardial injury," said Dr. Braun to the head nurse.

The heart monitor I was strapped to beeped continuously and sounded like one long screech indicating elevated heart rate and blood pressure.

"He is going into respiratory failure," said the nurse.

When I arrived my Glasgow Comma Scale score for eye, motor and verbal response was 4-5-6, I also had a respiratory rate of 40 breaths per minute. My systolic blood pressure was 85 mmHg with my heat beating 134 beats per minute but I was deteriorating. Looking at the x-ray Dr. Braun pinpointed to the exact ribs that were damaged and determined that my left upper lung was partially collapsed and quickly transitioned to rescue mode. Her and her team made an incision and inserted a drainage tube in my left thoracic cavity since my lung cavity was filled up with blood. Next came the tracheal incubation with artificial ventilation. Stacy was a mess!

Thank God they curtained off the area. Ean was sitting just a few beds away. He got out of the accident with just a few scratches and was traumatized. This was adding insult to injury. My body was going into shock as my blood pressure dropped to 37mmHg. The level of blood increased in my thoracic cavity with increased drainage. The impact of the moose caused fractured ribs which in turn resulted in a left deep pulmonary laceration (DPL). Dr. Braun went in and clamped my left drainage tube. My condition was worsening, my shock state continued and the rapid fluid infusion and therapy did not improve my condition. Since the Coma scale was now reading 1-T-1 Dr. Braun decided to perform a Thoracotomy right in the emergency room a few beds away from Ean.

They did not put me under general anesthesia but I did not mind because I could not feel a thing. It was strange but I was enlightened. I could finally settle the longtime debate if asked. Although I could not physically feel my body, my mind felt for Ean and what he must have been going through, knowing the state I was in. This experience settled the long debate for philosophers, especially Aristotle, who pondered whether the mind was in the heart or brain. I could felt my heart in my mind even though I could not physically feel my body. I was in the ER for an hour and fifteen minutes before they transported me to an operating room. I was still alive.

I have to get out of here.

Ean and I just had a baby.

Ean needs me.

Tur needs me.

I have to get out of here.

I can't move.

I can't feel my body.

I feel my heart.

I always win.

Ean was sitting on the edge of the hospital bed with Tur in his arms when Brian walked into the ER. It was almost noon and Tur was hungry. He did not have much of his bottle this morning before we left the cottage. Brian approached the ER station.

"I'm here to see the family from this morning's accident," said Brian to the male nurse at the station as he motioned to Ean.

"Go ahead," said the nurse as he grabbed onto a clip board to check in on a patient.

As Brian approached, Ean placed a baby wipe over his shoulder then Tur and patted lightly onto his back. He gently rocked up and down as he patted. Tur let out a burp. Brian moved closer to the bed and stood beside it. There were no chairs in the ER to sit on to deter visitors from lingering. Brian was about to speak when Ean's cell phone rang. Ean put Tur back in the car seat on the bed and reached into his pocket to retrieve the phone. Tur began to cry, so Brian reached over to the car seat and gently rocked it. Ean turned to Brian and smiled. The rocking motion quieted Tur. Ean pulled out his phone and placed it to his ear.

"Thank you," said Ean as he looked up at Brian.

Brian motioned to Ean that it was OK.

"Hello," said Ean.

"I got your message. Is everything alright?" asked Erica.

The male nurse saw Ean answer his phone and went over to him.

"No phones allowed in the ER," snapped the nurse.

"Hold on," said Ean as he turned to Brian.

"Would you mind?" asked Ean.

"Go ahead. I'll watch him," said Brian.

Ean walked out of the ER to the hospital corridor.

"Stacy is still in surgery and I haven't received an update from the doctor," said Ean.

"Is he conscious?" asked Erica.

"He's been unconscious since this morning," said Ean.

"Oh, God," said Erica.

"The car was totaled and I need you to come and get me and Tur," said Ean.

"How is the baby?" asked Erica.

"He's fine. There is not a scratch on him. I was actually in the middle of feeding him and the trooper who helped us is here to speak with me. Can you come get us? I don't want to take the train," asked Ean.

"I'll leave in a few minutes," said Erica.

"You can go straight to the house. They are keeping us overnight for observation. You still have your key?" asked Ean.

"Yeah, thanks for reminding me, it's in my drawer," said Erica.

"I love you," said Erica.

"I love you too," said Ean has he closed his phone and walked back into the ER.

Brian is still softly rocking Tur in the car seat.

"I'm sorry about that," said Ean.

"It's quite alright. You have been through a lot today," said Brian.

"How can I help you?" asked Ean.

"My job requires a full report of the incident," said Brian.

"That animal came out of nowhere," said Ean.

"We have seen an increase in moose-vehicle accidents this year. It is more common during the rut. Those animals are so tall that a vehicle can pass under them resulting in them going through windshields and over roofs as you experienced this morning," said Brian.

"By the time I saw the moose, it was too late. We usually see deer on the road and can detect them in the distance by their eyes," said Ean.

Brian glanced into the car seat and stopped rocking when he noticed Tur was asleep.

"The eyes of a moose are usually way above the headlights on a car and their color makes them undetectable, especially at dawn," said Brian as Dr. Braun approached them.

"How are you and the baby doing?" asked Dr. Braun.

"We're fine. How is Stacy?" asked Ean.

"Well, you know he has blunt chest trauma that caused a pulmonary laceration which required an emergency thoractomy. He is still in critical condition," said Dr. Braun.

"Has he woken up?" asked Ean.

"He is still unconscious; however, his vitals are much better. Stacy's body is still in shock. We are doing all that we can for him. Do you know who is his medical proxy?" asked Dr. Braun.

"I am, but I don't have the paper with me," said Ean as he looked to the floor.

Dr. Braun looked at Brian and gave a concerned grin.

"Do you have any questions?" asked Dr. Braun.

"No," said Ean.

"There should be a room opening upstairs soon for you. Please let me know if you need anything," said Dr. Braun as she rubbed Ean's upper arm and then moved on to the next patient.

"Will you both need a ride home tomorrow?" asked Brian.

"My sister is coming up tonight," said Ean as the male nurse approached holding Ean's and Tur's charts.

"We have a room ready for you upstairs. We will keep the baby overnight in the nursery. Please gather your belongings and come with me," said the nurse.

Brian grabbed onto the car seat and lifted Tur to help assist Ean. Brian's help and attention was comforting to Ean.

"I don't know when my sister will be able to get here, we can use the lift," said Ean as the four of them headed to the elevator.

The nurse first brought Ean to his room then took Tur.

"Make yourself at home. There are pajamas in the drawer. Just ring the bell if you need anything. You can pick him up after you are discharged," said the nurse as he took the car seat from Brian and carried Tur out of the room.

"I'll let you get settled in. My day begins early so I should be here early to bring you home," said Brian as he headed for the door.

"I will see you then. Thanks for everything," said Ean as Brian left the room.

The next morning Ean was awakened by a team of doctors led by Dr. Braun. The doctors huddled around Dr. Braun outside of his room while she briefed them on his case then lead them into the room knocking on the door as they entered.

"Good morning! How are you today?" asked Dr. Braun.

A nurse walked in who was monitoring Ean's vitals all night.

"Any difficulties?" asked Dr. Braun.

"None at all, he's fine," said the nurse.

Dr. Braun approached Ean and felt around his neck and shoulders then took her stethoscope and listened to his heart.

"Deep breaths," she ordered.

The team of doctors just stood around and watched.

"Do you want to go home today?" asked Dr. Braun.

"Yes," said Ean.

When the doctor was through she turned to the team.

"Any questions?"

They all shook their heads. The nurse stood by the door waiting for Dr. Braun's instructions.

"How's Stacy?" asked Ean.

Dr. Braun turned around to face him.

"I will come back to speak with you."

Dr Braun turned to the nurse.

"He can be discharged today," said Dr Braun as she raised and dropped her head.

The doctors started to leave the room as the nurse followed behind them waiting for them all to clear out. When everyone left the room Ean climbed out of the bed, grabbed a towel and headed for the bathroom. When Brian arrived Ean was all dressed and sat up on the bed waiting for Dr. Braun to come back to speak with him. Brian walked into the room.

"Were you able to get some rest?" asked Brian.

"I was having some trouble. The nurse gave me an *Ambien* last night. It helped. The doctor gave me the green light. We can head out soon. I'm just waiting for her to come back to update me on Stacy's condition," said Ean.

Brian took a seat beside the room's only window. He pulled off his hat and held it on his lap. Ean was able to get a good look at him and realized how blue his eyes were. He thought about complimenting him but refrained when Dr. Braun walked into the room. She seemed surprised that Brian is there.

"He's ready to go home today," she said.

"How is Stacy?" asked Ean.

"As I explained yesterday, we had to place him on the respirator. You know he is in a coma. We are keeping him in the Intensive Care Unit (ICU) until he is breathing on his own. There is also the possibility of paralysis. He is not physically responding to tests. We will continue to monitor him closely. We do have all of your contact information," said Dr. Braun.

The frown on Ean's face grew deeper.

"Is he improving?" asked Ean.

"It is too soon to tell. We are doing our best with him, I assure you," said Dr. Braun.

"Can I take the baby home?" asked Ean.

"Do you have support at home?" asked Dr. Braun.

"My sister is staying with me," said Ean.

"Good. The baby will also be discharged today. I don't see any problems," said Dr. Braun.

Why? Why? I asked myself was everything fine with a man raising a child just as long as there is a female involved? Then I remembered my past conversation with Ms. Green when I was in Kindergarten and her telling me mothers provide something special.

"There is one thing; however, I do need Stacy's healthcare proxy," said Dr. Braun.

"I will bring them in soon," said Ean.

When Dr. Braun finished her update and left she sent the nurse in with Ean's discharge papers. Ean quickly signed the forms and gathered himself together.

"Do you have everything?" asked Brian.

"I didn't have anything. I just need to get Tur," said Ean.

Before picking up Tur, Ean had a prescription for *Ambien* filled at the hospital pharmacy then came to the ICU with Brian to check on me. I really did not want him to see me in the condition I was in. As Dr. Braun explained, there was a respirator and feeding tube sticking out of my mouth as I laid on an incline strapped to two separate monitors. The ICU is designed so that the most critical patients' rooms were directly opposite the nurse's station. The doors to my room were both wide open and a video camera was on me all the time. There also was a nurse stationed outside the room keeping an eye on my vitals. Ean slowly approached the door and stopped halfway into the room. Brian stood behind him. He just stood there looking at me. There was nothing he could do. I could feel my heart. Not my body just my heart. My throat was sore. I coughed gagging on the tubes. After ten minutes Brian mimicked Dr. Braun's signature gesture and rubbed Ean's upper arm.

"I think we should pick up Tur," said Brian.

Tears ran down Ean's face. He did not say a word as Brian gripped onto his upper arm and guided him out of the room. They both left the ICU and headed for the nursery to pick up Tur. By the time they reach the nursery Ean had come back from a state of dissociation. Dissociation is one of Ean's coping skills. The average person dissociates occasionally to handle stress; however, this was Ean's strongest defense mechanism. He did not talk to Brian on the way to the nursery. When they entered the floor and approached the nurse's station his flight from reality helped him regroup and demand that he have his child. Ean signed Tur out and took him in his car seat. Brian did not interfere. His training on victims taught him that control needed to be placed back with the victim and Ean showed that he tried to take control over the situation. Brian was happy that he could help. After Ean and Brian picked up Tur from the nursery the three of them left the hospital and headed for the cottage.

# Part II

# Solitude

# Chapter IV

## Lonely Nights

"Hello."

"This is Mark calling from the DEC. I'm trying to reach Stacy."

"He is in the hospital, what is this about?"

"He was in an accident with a bull moose."

"I am aware of that. What do you want?"

"I am required by law to let him know that state law would allow him to obtain a permit from a law enforcement officer to keep a moose carcass since his vehicle was damaged by it."

"We are not interested."

"Well if you change your mind you can get the permit from Trooper Flannery, he gave me your number."

"Is the moose dead?"

"No, we have not caught it. We were unable to track it since its GPS fell off during the accident. When found and if euthanized, you can sell it for some compensation for the damage to your vehicle."

"No thanks, we have insurance."

"We will most likely put it down since it has made a nuisance of itself and injured life."

"Thanks for calling but like I said, we are not interested.

"If you change your mind you can just give me a call," said Mark as Ean hung up the phone.

Ean grabbed the mouse of his computer to return to the psycho-social assessment he was typing before Mark called. Ean looked down at the open file in front of him and read the progress note. He was still working on the backlog of MICA clients his supervisor assigned to him. As Ean finished up the report, Saudi came over to his desk.

"Hello, Mr. Ean. How's your honey and the baby,"

"They're holding their own."

"How are you doing?"

"I'm having a hard time focusing. I think I'm going to use my Family Medical Leave time."

"That's twelve weeks. It's been very busy here."

"With Stacy out of work I really should be coming back full time. There is just too much going on. He's all the way up north and I have the baby."

"Just take one thing at a time."

"I know. I need to get a car to get back and forth."

"Why did you come in today?"

"I'm just in for half a day to clear off my desk before I take the time off."

"I don't think the boss is going to be too happy."

"I know but there is nothing else I can do. I need to be able to get back and forth to the hospital. Let me go in and get this over with, wish me luck."

"I'll talk to you later," said Saudi as Ean got up from his desk and went into his supervisor's office.

An hour later Ean arrived at Erica's house by taxi. He planed on taking Tur up north with him but had no means of transportation. Ean thought to ask Erica if he could use her car to get up north. When he walked through the door Erica had Tur in her arms wearing a blue bib. Erica lead Ean into the living room where she had Tur's basinet set up and a blanket sprawled in front of the television. The local forecast was being announced on the news. A severe ice storm was predicted to hit the North Country in a few hours. The weatherman indicated that icy rain and sleet for the North Country would begin falling soon. Erica did not know what Ean's plans were for the evening.

"May I borrow your car for a few days?"

"Sure, you need it for work?"

"Actually, my supervisor allowed me to take family medical leave time. I have about twelve weeks off starting today."

"That's great."

"I'm taking Tur up north with me tonight."

"You can't travel tonight. Didn't you hear there is a storm coming in?"

"We'll be fine."

"Why don't you stay tonight and leave in the morning?"

"I want to be up north tonight so I can be at the hospital in the morning."

"You shouldn't be traveling with the baby in this weather."

"Can you please get him ready?"

"Why don't you leave him here with me until the storm passes and I will bring him up?"

"I made up my mind."

"In good conscience I can't lend you the car," said Erica as she turned away.

"Come on, we'll be fine. Please get him ready."

Erica stood still without moving then turned to Ean. Tur began to squirm in her arms as his head bobbled forward and back. Erica let out a breath. She knew how stubborn both of them were. Erica left to get the baby ready. As Ean sat on the sofa his eyes strained at the television that displayed a winter storm warning advisory that flashed below the screen as the news reporter read the headlines. Fifteen minutes later Erica brought Tur back into the living room fully dressed in a winter thermal body suit.

"He ate just before you got here. You may need to change his diaper."

"I'll take care of it."

"The storm will be in soon. Are you sure you don't want to stay tonight?"

"I need to get up there."

"Call me when you get in," said Erica as she handed Tur over to Ean.

Ean took Tur and headed for the garage.

Erica darted ahead of Ean and opened the door. Erica stood in the doorway as Ean put Tur in the back seat of her Explorer. Then she went over to the work bench and reached up to the wall behind it and pulled a set of keys off the wall and walked over to Ean.

"You're going to need these," said Erica as she went over to the work bench, picked up the garage door remote and pressed the button.

The garage opened.

"I'll get it back to you soon," said Ean as he hoped into the driver seat of the car, turned on the ignition and drove out of the garage as Erica closed the garage door and went back into the house.

Ean headed north on I-87 as snow and sleet began to fall. Tur was nestled in his car seat sound asleep. The weather forecaster predicted that the snow would not begin to fall until a few hours later, but it was not the first time the local weatherman got the Doppler forecast wrong. As Ean continued north the sky opened. The amount of flakes and sleet that fell tripled. Ean reached up to the steering wheel and adjusted the speed of the windshield wipers as the heavy slush that fell accumulated. A small cloud of vapor exited Ean's mouth each time he exhaled. The window began to fog up and prevented him from seeing the road ahead. Slowing down the car, Ean extended his arm in front of him and pulled the tip of his coat over his hand and wiped the window. He reached down to turn up the temperature and increased the

speed of the fan. The side view mirror was also
becoming covered with clumps of the mixture that
was whirled around. Ean opened the driver side
window to clear off the mirror. The winds whirled
inside the car and created a helicopter sound
effect. As he reached outside the car window with
his left hand the car swerved and Ean quickly
pulled his arm back in and grabbed the steering
wheel to get control of the vehicle. Sweat formed
on his brow and a drop of perspiration fell from
under his right arm pit. He continued to proceed
at an unsafe speed. The designated speed limit
sign he passed read sixty-five miles per hour.

Ean hated driving. He read the driver safety
manual at least six times, including each of the
three times he took the defensive driving course.
No matter how much training he still was not
comfortable behind the wheel. Ean put on the
hazard lights and moved over to the far right lane.
Cars flew by leaving behind splashes of slush on
his windshield. As Ean preceded north a snow
removal truck entered the highway, with its shovel
lifted in the air. It lowered the shovel as it made
its way onto the highway. Ean slowed the Explorer
down to allow the truck to enter ahead of him. He
creped up behind the truck as rockets of salt
pellets came crashing under the Explorer and
bounced up hitting the windshield. He slowed the
car and followed the truck for the next few exits
until it reached a detour. It was early evening and
the little sunlight out was quickly descending into
the night. The wintry mix created coats of ice on
power lines. There were no lights on in the houses
as he passed the next three northern towns. The
freezing rain continued to fall as Ean followed the

long line of cars exiting the highway detour to Route 9 as he and Tur made their way to the camp.

When Ean finally got to the camp he unloaded Tur and his changing bag from the car and got him inside. Ean turned up the thermostat and changed himself and Tur into lounging clothes. Tur was due for a diaper change. After he changed Tur's diaper, he placed him in the nursery crib and propped up a bottle in his mouth. As Tur drank the bottle, Ean went into the living room and turned on the television to channel 5 news and checked phone messages. The answering machine was flashing the number two. Ean pressed the play button and heard Mark's voice.

"I am calling from the DEC, please give us a call when you get this message. We are calling in regards to the incident that occurred on I-87. We can be reached at...," said Mark as Ean pushed the delete button.

The machine went onto the next message.

"It's me. Call me when you get in," said Erica as Ean hit the delete button.

Tur began to cry and Ean immediately rushed into the nursery to get him. Ean lifted Tur from the crib and brought him into the living room. Ean sat down on the recliner in front of the television and gently rocked him as he placed the bottle in his mouth.

"I know, I'm tired too. Get some sleep my little boy?"

Lin of channel 5 news appeared on the screen.

"There was another sighting of a large male bull moose on the road this evening. We brought you the story just a few days ago that a family of three was injured from a run in with a moose on this same exact highway. Early fall is what they call the rut, the breeding season for moose in northern New York, which explains why they may sometimes be seen on the road. Their presence has become more common. In less than two weeks three moose have been killed on North Country roads and two separate families injured. One of the accident victims is still in the hospital. With the change in the winter season there should be less moose out and about. Reporting live from I-87, now back to the studio," said Lin as Ean picked up the remote and turned off the television.

Ean lifted himself and Tur who was sound asleep out of the chair and carried him back into the nursery. He placed Tur in the crib and turned on the baby monitor and nightlight by Stacy's desk. As he turned to walk away from the desk the key in the drawer glistened from the light and caught his attention. Ean looked down at the desk drawer and pulled the chair from the desk and sat down. He glanced up at the wedding picture of him and Stacy in Ottawa on the shelf of the desk and then down at the key in the drawer. Ean pulled on the drawer. When it did not open he turned the key and opened it. There laid Stacy's journal with the picture of Da Vinci's *Embryo in Uterus* on the cover. Ean pulled out the journal. The journal had an envelope and a few loose pages stuffed in it. He removed the envelope and pages from the journal and placed them on the desk. Ean opened the cover of the journal and began to read.

*Mooers, New York*
*September 8th*


*Dear Son:*
*When you read this you will be a man as I am now and I truly hope you understand. I am leaving you this story so you know that your journey into this world was an act of love. I cannot tell you your mother's story because that is something only she can do. My story is that I was a desperate and foolish young man who wanted so much to be connected: however, I ran in the other direction separating myself from my family trying to make it on my own in the world without the help of those who came before me. While I was in college I began to understand relationships and did not understand my true sexuality or what I wanted from life. Yale was a school of fraternities and frat boys. I wanted so much to be part of something and someone so I joined a fraternity with my roommate who was my best friend. I joined because I was conflicted about my sexuality and enjoyed being with my roommate. Finding out who I am is a whole other story. How do you fit in? Like every other fraternity, one must be initiated into it to be a member. Ever year when new recruits apply their initiation ritual is chosen out of a little book called "100 Things to Do Before You Die." The 100 things, ranging from learning a new language to practicing yoga, are put into a lottery and then selected. When the head fraternity brother selected the task for the new initiates it was sperm donation. This was one of the fraternities' favorite choices because it helped raise money for the fraternity to fund the kegs to*

*celebrate the new initiates. It truly is not that simple. Overall, you are the result of my need to survive. Without you I could not live. My part of you was placed in a tube and deposited for a one time donation of fifty dollars; however, your life is worth more than that to me. Doing what I did allowed me to be with others and share life. I never thought I would have the chance to raise you. Part of the fraternity pact was that we could never have contact with who we helped create. I defied my brothers and when filling out the paperwork I did not choose to remain anonymous because I wanted to know if you, a part of me, existed. I leave this story for you. When you are a man and finish reading this story, I hope you understand. Finally, please accept Ean's love because he is also your father. With all my love.*

> *Your father,*
> *Stacy*

Ean stopped reading when he got to the bottom of the first page and looked at the envelope and loose page that was tucked inside the journal. The loose sheet was a child like drawing of a figure of a man made up of shapes and words. Inside the envelope was a letter addressed to Stacy and two pictures of a newborn infant. Ean began to read the letter from Claudia. She looked different than her mug shot and the photo attached to her rap sheet back at his office. In the letter Claudia gave her current number and asked Stacy to call her. Ean lifted the letter closer to his face and read it, then lowers in onto the table. He picked up the two pictures of the infant and easily recognized the child in the photos. The pictures were of Tur a day after his delivery. One photo showed him wrapped in the clear plastic tray newborns are held in and the second photo showed Claudia, a cocoa-colored Persian woman lying on a hospital bed with a face that was physically drawn and tired looking with dark circles under her eyes holding Tur. Ean folded the letter up and placed it back in the envelope with the two pictures. He tucked the envelope into the journal and put it back where he found it. He slowly closed the drawer and turned the key. The metal loop the key was attached to dangle from the key as Ean got up from the chair and walked over to the wall where *l'orignal* hung. Ean cried as he reached up and began to pull on the moose head trying to detach it from the wall. Ean pulled and tugged but the mount was too strong. Ean turned away from *l'orignal* and walked over to the crib. He looked down on Tur as tears well up in his eyes. He stared at Tur as the tears streamed down his face. Ean wiped his eyes as he turned from the crib and left the room.

The next morning Ean walked into the intensive care unit carrying Tur in his car seat. He approached the nurse's station. Dr. Braun was standing behind the counter reviewing a patient's chart with a nurse.

"Doctor!"

Dr. Braun turned to Ean.

"Just one moment, please," said the doctor as she turned back to the nurse to resume her conversation.

"You know the baby is not allowed in the unit," said a nurse sitting behind the desk typing into a computer terminal.

Dr. Braun walked over to Ean as he backed away from the counter ignoring the nurse's comment.

"How are you both doing?" asked the doctor as she gave Ean her signature touch to his upper arm.

"We're fine. How is he?"

"We tried to reach you this morning. He came out of the coma last night demanding to see you."

Ean looked down the hall in the direction of the room he had last seen Stacy in with Trooper Flannery.

"We moved him to another room, but before we go to see him you should know that patients in his condition can be very emotional. As you know he has been through much and is dealing with the loss of time and movement."

"I understand."

"He is breathing on his own. We removed the respirator this morning so he has some soreness to his throat. I scheduled him for physical therapy starting tomorrow. More activity is needed so we can see if we can get other parts of his body moving again. He is able to move his head, right arm and hand. Do you have any questions?"

"When do you think he will be able to come home?"

"He's a strong man and he came out of the coma with a vengeance. I would say in a couple of weeks. We want to monitor him for a few days until he gets his full strength back. His lungs and chest look like they are healing very well. Let's go see him," said Dr. Braun as she and Ean walked down the hall.

As they left the nurse's station the nurse at the computer terminal glared at Ean. I was sleeping when they entered my room. Dr. Braun turned to Ean.

"Let him sleep."

"Do we have to leave?"

"No, just let him wake-up on his own," said Dr. Braun as she left the room.

Ean walked over to a florescent lime green foam chair by the bed and sat down with the car seat on his lap. He placed the car seat on the floor beside the chair and took off his coat. As he draped the coat over the back of the chair the zippers' catch hit the metal leg of the chair and the sound of a chime rang out and woke up Tur. Tur began to cry. Ean lifted him up out of the car seat as I opened my eyes. Ean rocked Tur as he reached down for his bottle in the car seat.

"Shush! Daddy's sleeping."

I smiled as I watched Ean place the bottle in Tur's mouth and rock him gently. Tur sucked on the bottle and stopped crying. As Ean rocked Tur he looked up at me smiling at him.

"Hey," said Ean as he got up and leaned over the bed with Tur in his arms and kissed me on the cheek.

"Water!"

Ean went over to a pitcher of ice water on a table by the other side of the bed and poured me a cup as he held Tur and brought the water over to me.

With Tur in one arm Ean lifted the cup of ice water to my mouth. I slowly lifted my right arm to grab onto the cup. My hand trembled. I drink a gulp of water and begin to cough uncontrollably.

The heart and blood pressure monitor beeped continuously as the red digital numbers display increased then lowers.

"Are you alright?"

"Yes."

"It's good to see you. I missed you," said Ean as he took the cup of water and put it on the table beside the bed.

"I missed you too."

"The doctor said your lungs and chest are healing well and she wants to get you in physical therapy right away."

"I can't move."

Tears streamed down my face.

"I know. We'll be fine," said Ean as he wiped my tears.

"I want to go home."

"You will be home soon enough. I took time off so I will be with you."

"How am I going to take care of you and Tur."

"Don't worry. We will be fine," said Ean as the tears continued to drop from my eyes.

"Come now," said Ean as he walked back over to the table and took a clean cloth.

Ean walked over to a sink in the far corner of the room and wet the cloth then came back to the bed still with Tur in his arms and wiped my face.

"Everything is going to work out fine."

I stopped crying.

"My job!"

"Don't worry. Lavonda informed your boss."

Ean put the wet cloth on the table then sat back down on the chair as Rona and Aton approach the doorway. Rona walked straight into the room followed by Aton and immediately came to my bedside.

"Hi Mom! Hi Dad!"

"Oh honey," said Rona as she reached over the bed and kissed me. Tears began to well up in my eyes again.

Aton did not say a word. He walked around my mother and grabbed on to my leg. I could see him do it but could not feel a thing. Aton backed up against the wall and remained in his position for the rest of the visit. My parents did not acknowledge Ean or Tur until I point out to them that they were in the room.

"How are you?" asks Rona.

"Fine, thank you," said Ean as my father nodded his head in Ean's direction.

"Mom, I'm paralyzed."

Rona did not say anything for a moment as my father just stared at the lower part of my hospital bed. She turned to look at my father who just stood there staring with a blank look on his face. Rona then did as she always did. She went into a story to explain the difficult situation I was in.

"Did I ever tell you about the story of your grandmother?"

"Which?"

She had tons of them.

"Your grandmother always taught that everything happens for a reason. Your grandmother was just a young girl back then. She was sent away to the camps with her younger siblings during the war like the rest of our ancestors. One morning all the children were gathered together. They were not fed a breakfast that day. By noontime many of the children were crying out of hunger. They weren't fed much in the camps. The children were separated into groups and led outside the camp. They were made to hike a few miles. Your grandmother explained as the children walked they reached down and pulled up plants and grass from the side of the road to nourish their weak bodies. Your grandmother and another girl were the oldest of the bunch. She helped guide her siblings, your relatives, along the road to their destination. When they finally arrived at where they were being taken, the children were instructed to lay in a freshly dug ditch. The soldiers shot off their guns to scare the children who immediately lay down as instructed. Your grandmother carried her infant sister to that place. The soldiers that led the children to that place ordered your grandmother to put the infant in the ditch with the rest of the children. At first she refused. They pointed a gun at her and gave her a final order. She cried as she laid the child down in the arm of another child in the ditch whose arms were too weak to support the child. She ran into the arms of the other girl her age. As the both of them cried soldiers opened fired on the children. That day you grandmother witnessed the death of many children and until the time of her death she asked the question of God why she was still alive. Before she died she made peace with God. You will too."

Ouch! Yes, make my peace with God. That will solve my current dilemma. My parents did not stay long. The highlight of their visit was when I told them our child's name.

"You named him Tur?" she asked but did not show any interest to look at him. Because she could not deal with the reality of the child, Rona went into another story, making it relevant to her way of life.

"Yes, he was named after..."

"You don't have to tell us. We know the story of the Arba'ah Turim and The Four Rows. It was written by Rabbi Jacob ben Asher between the twelve and thirteen hundreds."

"Yaakov ben Asher, who lived in Spain," my father chimed in.

His first words since he got here.

"Tur covers the Jewish religious law. The four rows of the Tur represent the four jewels of the High Priest's breastplate, "The Path of Life," "Teach knowledge," "The rock of the Helpmate," and "The breastplate of Judgment," said Rona as my father listened closely to make sure she got it right.

The talk of law excited him so much that he decided to join the discussion.

"The Tur is the most widely used structure of law codes and organized interpretations that were followed in lands outside of Israel. Foreign lands without a temple!"

Ean and I remained silent and took it all in as they went on and on. I had enough of these lessons when I was in the Yeshiva. Tur was sound asleep. I said a prayer of thanks to God that the nurse who was at the computer terminal when Ean arrived interrupted them as she made her rounds to let all the visitors know that visiting hours for the morning were over. When she entered the room she made it a point to address Ean directly not looking at my parents.

"Morning visiting hours are now over. Babies are not allowed in the ICU! If you come back with the baby we will ask you to leave," said the nurse as she turned around and left the room.

"We better get going then," said Rona.

Both my parents came over to the bed and kissed me goodbye.

"I love you," I said.

No response. They left without looking back.

Ean put his jacket on and tucked Tur in the car seat and headed out after they left.

"I'll see you soon."

He kissed me and then held the car seat up to the bed. I reach out to touch Tur with my good hand as he slept. Ean walked out of the room carrying Tur.

~ ~ ~ ~

I did make it home three whole weeks later. Ean was advised by Dr. Braun to attend a workshop offered by the hospital called "*How to Live With and Care for a Disabled Family Member*". My situation required that changes be made to the camp so that it was conducive to my condition. A new ramp had to be installed in the front of the house. My condition also required a special medical bed with an electrical lift and pulley. The bathroom also needed to be supplied with additional supportive devices that would help me maneuver around. To the doctor's mystery I was not a full quadriplegic. I somehow still had the functioning of my right arm. It was a blessing but still difficult because I was left handed. Dr. Braun told me there would be a lot of relearning and I was up to it. Going home energized me. I could not give up and I was determined to catch up to where I had left off. Like my father I too have a passion for law and am unwavering in getting back to the courtroom to provide for my family, knowing it was not going to be easy. Due to the weather we were unable to begin the exterior construction on the camp to build the ramp so the hospital transported me by ambulance in a wheelchair. They had some difficulty getting me up the stairs and into the house, but I made it home. Ean reorganized the furniture in the living room to allow for more space for the wheelchair. The transporters wheeled me straight into the bedroom and placed me in the bed. I had been in bed for weeks and wanted to get up and around.

"Can you help me?"

Ean went into the nursery to check on Tur then came back into the bedroom to help. He grabbed the wheelchair and put it near the side of the bed and locked the wheels in place. I bent my right arm behind me and attempted to lift my body.

"Wait a minute," said Ean as he came to my aid.

He went over to the dresser and grabbed the hoisting sling and wrapped it around me. Ean swiveled my legs off the side of the bed and anchored me and lifted me off the bed and placed me in the chair like he was shown in his training. After lifting my legs and setting them in place he unlocked the chair and wheeled me into the living room.

"Are you hungry for lunch?"

"I'm starving."

The hospital breakfast this morning consisted of a small cup of coffee, apple juice, and bowl of oatmeal. Ean went into the kitchen and fixed a grilled cheese sandwich and a bowl of tomato soup made with milk just like I like it. When it was ready he wheeled me into the kitchen. The kitchen table and island have been pushed up against the wall. Ean locked me in place and we sat and ate lunch.

"I've been thinking about a schedule."

"What kind of schedule?"

"I'm thinking about a schedule for you and Tur."

"I don't need a schedule."

"But I do if I'm going to be taking care of you both."

"Did they teach you that in your class?"

"Actually, they did."

The sandwich was grilled to perfection and the temperature of the soup is just right.

"I think you know what you're doing," I said.

In that split second reality sank in. I was dependant on him.

"Make Tur your priority not me."

"I'll try to meet his needs first."

"What happens when nature calls for the both of us?"

Ean looked at me without expression.

"Honey, I'm joking with you."

"I know we'll be fine."

He kept saying that, and I got the impression that he really truly did not believe it. The repetition was an attempt to convince himself that everything was going to be all right. Three weeks later Ean had it all figured out, so he thought. As planned, he developed a routine and placed us on a schedule making sure all of Tur's needs were met before assisting me. Ean set Tur up in the playpen after breakfast. Tur settled in and stayed staring at the television screen as Ean popped in a *Baby Einstein* DVD. No matter how many times the disc played Tur is fascinated by the vivid colors, classical music and stimulating sounds that come from the television. Once Ean saw Tur was focused, he wheeled me into the bathroom and hoisted me into the shower. As I sat Ean turned on the water and tested the temperature. Ean closed the shower curtain and pulled the level to redirect the water out of the shower spout. The water came crashing down over my body. Once fully wet, Ean shut off the water and grabbed a wash cloth and lathered it up with body wash. After scrubbing my body completely he restarted the water and tested the temperature before he redirected the water over my body. I always wondered what it was like to go through a car wash without a car and after a few weeks I learned. Ean was gentle when he began but I could sense that this routine of washing me had now become a chore. If only I was not in this condition. There seemed to be something pressing on Ean's mind. Everyday our conversations were becoming shorter.

"How are you today?"

"I'm fine."

"What would you like to eat today?"

He did not dare to ask what I wanted to do because there was nothing much I could do but sit in the chair.

"Maybe a PB&J for lunch," I said as Tur began to whine then cry.

Ean reached for a towel and draped it over my shoulders.

"Give me a second."

Ean left the room to tend to Tur. One minute later Tur stopped crying. Three minutes later Ean was back in the bathroom drying my body off. He placed a dry towel on the seat of the wheelchair then lifted me up and out of the shower and onto the dry towel. Ean covered me with the damp towel and rolled me into the bedroom to get dressed.

As he dressed me I dared to ask.

"Is everything OK?"

"Yeah, I'm just a bit tired."

"Is that it?"

"I've been thinking about going back to work."

"We have some money saved."

"I know but it won't last forever. Besides, I am over the allotted time for the Family Medical Leave Act and my boss won't hold my job forever."

"My disability payments will be coming in soon."

"That's not enough."

"Don't worry, we'll be fine."

I gave it back to him. My pent up aggression from the accident was coming out. If he heard his own words, maybe reality would sink in.

"Maybe we can get someone from the hospital to help out."

"I don't want an aide in here. I don't like the idea of strangers coming into the house."

"Maybe Erica can come up and help out. You know how much she loves Tur."

He seems relieved when I suggested that his sister come up, but there is something else Ean was not telling me.

Early afternoon while Tur and I napped Ean picked up the phone to call Erica. He stayed in the living room holding the receiver in his hand. The phone started to beep to indicate the receiver was not docked. Ean hung up the phone then picked up the receiver again and dialed Erica's number. After three rings Leo answered.

"Hey how's it going? Is my sister there?"

"Let me get her."

Ean started to fiddle with the phone. He did not know if Erica was still upset with him for taking Tur the night of the storm. He never called her back and hadn't been in touch with her since.

"Hello."

Erica's voice was cold. Leo told her who it is.

"Hi sis it's me."

There was a short pause.

"How are things?"

"Things are well. Stacy is home."

"How are you managing?"

"OK, I guess."

"How's my nephew?"

"He's getting bigger every day. Would you like to come up and see him?"

Erica's voice softened.

"That would be nice."

"Pack a bag and stay the week. We miss you."

"I'm sorry for being so stubborn and taking Tur away. I know how much you love him."

"I've missed you guys, too."

"I really need your help."

Erica paused again.

"Never use a child as a pawn. It only hurts the child in the end."

Ean was silent.

"I'll be there on Friday."

"We were thinking about getting an aide in to help, but I don't like the idea of having a stranger in the house."

"You have to get over your fears."

"I thought it would be better if you were here instead. You're so good with Tur."

"I'm going to have to talk with Leo about that. He was getting a little jealous with all the time I was spending with Tur."

"He wants to be your only baby."

"Yeah, he's so sweet."

"I really need to talk to you about something."

"What is it?"

"I can't talk now but I found out something about Tur's biological parents."

"It's not anything bad is it?"

Tur began to cry.

"It depends on how you look at it. However, I need to confirm the story before I repeat it. Let's just say I was speechless when I found out."

"What's going on?"

"Listen, Tur is crying I need to get to him. We'll talk on Friday. See you then."

"Love you," said Erica, as Ean hung up the phone and ran into the nursery.

Ean picked up Tur's bottle and nestled it on top of a pillow between the wall of the crib and mattress placing it in Tur's mouth. Tur gave a couple of sucks to the bottle then began to cry. Ean felt the bottom of his diaper and realized he needed to be changed. He changed the soiled diaper and adjusted Tur in the crib by again propping his bottle up on his pillow. Tur quieted down and drifted off to sleep. Ean looked over to the desk in the room where he sat reading my journal a few weeks ago and was immediately drawn to the drawer where he had replaced my intimate thoughts. He stood still just looking at the drawer trying to resist learning more. He could not control his desires and approached the desk. Ean sat down, turned on the desk light and opened the drawer. He pulled out the journal and stopped for a moment and listened to hear if I was awake. He could only hear Tur as he deeply inhaled and exhaled between sucks of the bottle. Ean placed the journal on the desk and began to read where he left off.

Life came full circle for that moment in time. The creative force in the universe had directed Ean to sit in my place to begin preparing him to pick up in time where I left off. Ean's eyes shifted from left to right. His vision glided across the pages of the journal. He read the last words I wrote prior to the accident: "*I went over to the desk and pulled out my journal to continue documenting our time with Tur in the cabin and when I was done I slipped the journal back into the drawer, closed it and turned the key...Before I left the room I did, however, effortlessly glance at the baby monitor to ensure it was on before I headed off to bed.*"

After reading the last pages I had wrote Ean did the same but with one exception. Instead of going off to bed he instead returned to the living room and headed back to the phone. He lifted the receiver and dialed the number that was printed on the letter Claudia sent me. Ean memorized the number when he first read the letter. As he held the phone to his ear it rang on the other end. His heart pounded rapidly and his body warmed. After the third ring Claudia with her Parisian accent answered the phone. Ean could feel his gut as he visualized Claudia in the hospital bed holding Tur.

"This is Claudia."

Ean hesitated before he spoke.

"Hello!"

"Hi. You don't know me but I am caring for your son."

"Who is this? Stacy?"

"No, I'm Stacy's partner."

Now Claudia was silent.

"This is a man?"

"Yes."

"Then I don't understand."

"Stacy and I are married and we are Tur's foster parents. You signed the papers agreeing to Tur's Foster parent arrangement."

"Why are you calling? I thought Ean was female."

"I don't know. I guess I wanted to know if it was true."

"If what was true?"

"Can we meet?"

"I don't think so. Please don't call here again," said Claudia as she hung up the phone.

Ean slowly put down the receiver on the phone docking station and took in a deep breath. His heart was still pounding. After reading my journal the first time, he obviously did not accept the reality of the situation. Ean thought he knew all about me, but there were just some things that I held close to the heart and did not share with anyone, including him. Ean did not know that I could hear his every word or the sound of his body as he tossed and turned on the sofa as he tried to sleep at night. I liked to think that it was because he was not comfortable with our arrangement in sleeping alone that brought on his insomnia, and not what his mind was trying to process.

The next morning I could hear Ean awake and shuffle through the house getting Tur ready for the day. After cleaning the mess from the previous day, he came in to massage my body and go through our physical therapy routine before helping me take my shower. Although he massaged my body, lifted my arm and legs up and down and rotated them in a circular motion to increase my circulation, I began to develop small sores. Ean called a visiting nurse to check on me and she prescribed antibiotics and suggested that I go to see Dr. Braun if I got worse. When Ean walked into the room I could see that his young strong body was aging, wilting as the glow he once radiated was dulling. The rings around Ean's eyes were darkening. He knew my secret. However, he did not know that I knew he knew. Ean walked over to the bed and kissed me on the forehead.

"Are you ready for the day?"

"Yes."

"What would you like to do?"

He dared to ask.

"Sit outside."

I thought I would take it slow.

"It's still too cold out."

After my exercise routine Ean lifted me out of the bed with more aggression and less care as he dropped me into the wheelchair and yanked the harness from under me. I did not feel the burn but I knew the burn mark was there eating its way through my bed sore.

"Stop it!"

"What?"

"If you don't want to do this anymore you can go."

"Yeah, who's going to take care of you?"

"If you really want to leave, please don't stay on my account."

"Come on," said Ean as he held on to the wheelchair and lead me to the bathroom.

"How about you give me a sponge bath?"

I did not want to lose him. Ean was right again. My parents were too busy with their lives. My father was too busy with his law firm. My mother was too busy with her social events. Both constantly occupied with their religion, no correction, their way of life. How could I forget they are Jewish? Only God knows where my sister was. I haven't heard from her in years. Contact with Lavonda and all my associates ceased after the accident. Ean and Tur were the only two in my life.

"How about using the lavender body wash?"

I thought maybe the scent would relax him as they claimed it did in the commercials. As Ean washed my body his eyes focused on what he knew but could not bring himself to confront me. I was a lawyer who liked confrontation. Ean remained silent about what he knew. For the next five years he slept on the couch and cared for Tur and I with the help of Erica who came back into our lives that Friday. Even though Ean treated me like I was the one who was causing his distress and I felt guilty for it, I began to believe the real cause of his troubles was Tur.

When the day came to fully adopt Tur, I myself began to question whether or not we were doing the right thing. Jeanine told us that the process would take a few years. It gave us the time to decide if this was truly the right thing to do. It is for me, because Tur was my offspring. The years that would have passed with my not knowing if I had a child after I graduated from Yale would have been a thorn in my side. Now that I knew, I was relieved. I did not understand the true level of responsibility of having a child. Even with parenting classes, I was just out of the hospital when we received the call from Lavonda that Jeanine had contacted her stating that the agency was ready to allow our adoption of Tur. The agency had tried on numerous occasions to contact Claudia, to no avail. She never responded to their calls or correspondence. Claudia seemed to disappear. By not responding she forfeited her parental rights to Tur once again. Ean and I, with the help of Lavonda, petitioned the court and awaited a notice to appear for a custody hearing. We received the notice.

A week later we arrived at the family court building in Albany. Ean pushed me into the courtroom followed by Erica who held on to Tur. The courtroom was empty. The three of them took a seat directly in front of the judge's bench while I sat in my vehicle. We could hear the sound of people talking coming from an open door behind the jury box. The judge's clerk came into the courtroom to see who was there. She went back into the judge's chambers to get the judge. The doors of the courtroom opened and in walk Jeanine followed by Lavonda. Both of them approached us.

"You guys are ready to become permanent parents?" asked Jeanine.

"We've been waiting for this day for quite some time," I said as Ean smiled, looking a bit unsettled.

Judge Lamb and his clerk both came out of chambers and took their places in the courtroom. After the judge took his seat he looked at Lavonda.

"Counsel," said Judge Lamb.

"Your honor, the adoption before you today is docket number 09-0627. We are requesting that full custody be awarded to the current foster parents. Both foster parents are present here today and have cared for the child since birth. A representative of the adoption agency is also present here with us today," said Lavonda as she motioned to Jeanine.

The judge looked at Jeanine.

"Please approach," said Judge Lamb.

Jeanine approached the bench.

"Please state your name and agency," said the judge.

Jeanine responded to the judge's request then continued.

"Your honor, temporary custody for the child named Tur has been transferred to the foster parents and our agency is ready to transfer full parental and guardianship rights to the petitioners in court with us today."

The judge gave us all a look over then returned his attention to Lavonda.

"Have both biological parents received notice on termination rights and of this hearing today?" asked the Judge.

"Judge, a good faith effort has been made to reach the biological mother, with no response," said Lavonda.

"The biological mother had initially relinquished her rights during the initial foster care arrangement," said Jeanine.

"Your honor, the mother is currently involved in criminal litigation requiring a mandatory conditional discharge to treatment which I believe she is in violation of," said Lavonda.

"I see. What about the biological father?" asked Judge Lamb.

My heart thumped as I could see Ean turn his head to look at me out of the corners of his eyes.

"Your honor this child was conceived by artificial insemination. The biological father has not made any effort to contact the agency to find out if the child exists," said Lavonda.

"Well then, it is my opinion that the best interest of the child would be to award sole custody to the petitioners, so I am approving this adoption. A full order and final decree of adoption will be mailed to all parties within the next few days," said the Judge.

Lavonda thanked the judge and shook Jeanine's hand. Both of them approached us.

"Congratulations once again," said Jeanine.

"This is now final?" asked Ean.

"Yes, it is," said Lavonda.

We all thanked Judge Lamb and the clerk as we left the courtroom.

# Chapter V

# Sightings

Erica opened the front door as Tur came storming in. He was always charged when Erica picked him up from school. As Tur bolted through the front door he couldn't wait to show Ean his class project for the day.

"Eeen! Eeen!"

Tur shouted as he ran into the kitchen looking and pulling a along thread of red twine.

"Hey what have you got there?"

"Look!"

A blue diamond laid on the kitchen floor by the door attached to the thread.

"I made a kite."

"It files high," said Erica as she entered the kitchen.

Tur tugged on the thread and the blue diamond went flying in the air. A silver star that was glued to the kite glistened as the kite settled beside him.

"Boy can that kite fly!"

Tur smiled up at Ean. His arms stretched out in front of him as Tur jumped into them. Ean embraced him.

"How was school today?"

"Good."

"He received a silver star for his kite," said Erica.

"Thanks for getting him."

Ean looked down at Tur.

"You did very well today."

"Let's go get changed," said Erica.

"I have to go pick up some vitamins and orange juice."

"That's fine."

"Would you please check on Stacy? He said he is not feeling well. His skin looks like he is developing hives. The nurse changed his antibiotic again."

"Maybe he is having an allergic reaction?"

"The blotches look like Lyme disease, the nurse wasn't sure and said he might need testing."

"There are a lot of ticks up here."

"Take my car. I have you blocked in."

Erica handed Ean her keys. Ean walked over to the island and grabbed his cell phone and left. When Ean pulled out of the driveway Erica went to check on Tur. Tur was in his room struggling to take off his shirt. The crib was adjusted into a day bed. Tur sat on the edge of the bed trying to get his arm out of the shirt sleeve.

"Hey, you want help?"

"I can't get this off."

"I'll help you but let us first say hi to papa Stacy."

Erica pulled Tur's hand through the sleeve then held onto it and led him to see me. I had been in bed for the last two days, too tired to get up to bathe, so Ean did not see that the blotches that resemble hives had now darkened to resemble massive contusions over my body. Erica knocked on the door and as she entered the room she let go of Tur and walked over to the bed.

"We just want to say hello."

I was shivering uncontrollably. My body was covered with a heavy blanket and my forehead was covered in perspiration. Erica pulled the blanket back and when she lifted it she noticed the dark blotches covering my body.

"You're trembling. Are you OK?"

"Not really."

"I'll call the hospital," said Erica as she turned around and ran for the door.

She swooped up Tur on her way out and ran to the phone in the living room to call 911. Twenty minutes later the paramedics knock on the front door. Erica also tried to reach Ean on his cell phone but was unsuccessful. Each time she dialed his number she got the message:

"The subscriber you have called is unavailable at this time. Please try again later."

The phone did not allow her to leave a massage. Erica showed the paramedics into the bedroom. They took one look at me and began recording my vitals and decided I needed to be immediately taken to the hospital. They lifted me out of the bed and onto the wheelchair. Erica ran in Tur's room and got a bag ready. As the paramedics transferred me to the ambulance, Erica grabbed Ean's keys off the island in the kitchen and ran out to the car carrying Tur and the bag. She threw the bag in the back seat of the car. She stopped for a second realizing that Tur's car seat was in her vehicle. She sat Tur in the back of the car and strapped him in with the seatbelt, jumped in the driver's seat and headed after the ambulance. As she chased the ambulance she dialed Ean's number once again but there was still no answer.

Ean was at the local pharmacy picking up a bottle of vitamins. As he walked past the aisles in the store he looked up to find the sign for the vitamins. As he passed the aisle that held the toothpaste and mouthwash he saw Mark filling his basket with a pack of dental floss. When he first saw Mark he could not help but stop and stare. Mark was a bit taller than Ean and looked physically strong in his DEC uniform. Ean did not make the connection between Mark's DEC uniform and the call he received after I had the accident a few month ago. He was immediately attracted to the way Mark caressed the light brown hair that flowed over his face as he brushed his fingers through it pulling it back. Ean caught himself staring as Mark turned towards him and turned away. Mark caught Ean's reaction and smiled. Mark was excited that Ean seemed interested in him. They both were eager for attention. A store clerk passed Ean, carrying a basket of returns to be re-shelved.

"Where are the vitamins?"

"There in the next aisle."

Ean walked into the next aisle the clerk pointed out and stood before a huge selection not knowing which to choose. As he stood reading the labels Mark came into the aisle and walked up beside him. Mark reached around Ean for a bottle of *Centrum* and glanced at Ean's puzzled look on his face.

"Excuse me."

Ean stepped back and noticed Mark's closeness.

"Don't know which to get?"

"There are so many to choose from."

"These have a good consumer rating," said Mark as he lifted the bottle of pills toward Ean.

"They're for a sick friend."

"Zinc and B12 are important."

Mark stood beside Ean to help him make a choice.

"I sometimes have a hard time knowing what I want."

"Are you from around here? I've never seen you before."

"Yeah, I live just up the road."

"Do you have to get back to your sick friend?"

"Eventually."

"How about going for a drink sometime?"

"I've been sober for fifteen years."

"Then how about going for a coffee?"

"I can't, I have to get home."

"Maybe we can go dancing sometime?"

Ean smiled nervously. The last time he was asked to dance by a man it resulted in a Canadian marriage and an adopted child.

"Yeah, maybe."

"Take my number."

"Sure."

Ean pulled out his cell phone and hit the power button. Mark read off his number as Ean programmed it into the phone.

"And you are?"

"Mark."

"I'm Ean. It's nice to meet you."

"Call me soon, I could use the company."

Ean blushed. He was being polite but trying not to lead Mark on. Ean grabbed a bottle of the same vitamins Mark selected.

"Checking out?"

"Yeah," said Ean as he headed for the register.

Ean grabbed a box of *Altoids* breath mints from the counter and paid for his purchases and left the store. Mark followed right behind him.

"See you around."

"Later," said Ean as he smiled at Mark and waved goodbye.

Ean put the *Altoids* in his shirt pocket and threw the rest of his purchases in the passenger's seat and sat in the car. As he was about to turn on the ignition his cell phone rang.

"Hello," said Ean still smiling and feeling good from his interaction with Mark.

It's been years since he felt desired by anyone. Since my accident the only desire he felt from me did not feel at all like love. He became wedded to the duty to care for me so that any affection I expressed seemed to him to stems from his duty to me. I was more of a chore for him than anything.

"It's me. Listen."

Erica's tone was stressed.

"What going on?"

"Stacy is very sick."

"Did you call the doctor?"

"We're at the hospital. I've been trying to reach you."

"I'll be there soon," said Ean as he closed his cell phone, started the car and sped out of the parking lot.

When Ean arrived at the hospital he was given a pass to the ICU. Dr. Braun was outside my room talking to Erica. Tur was getting restless because he had not eaten a full meal. Erica bought cheese and crackers out of the vending machine in the lobby to feed him.

"I want to go home," said Tur as he wiped his eyes.

"We'll go home soon, I promise," said Erica as Ean approached them.

Dr. Braun had to explain everything all over.

"How is he?"

"It was good you brought him in."

"What's wrong?"

"It looks like he developed sepsis."

"What's that?"

"It's a severe blood infection. It looks like he developed it from the pressure wound on his back."

"I thought that was just a bed sore."

"The antibiotics are no longer working. The wound infected the blood."

107

"Can you switch the antibiotic?"

"He's been taking the strongest one we have."

"Is there anything else?" asked Erica as she lifted Tur and rocked him back and forth.

"Because of the infection his immune system was compromised and he developed Thrombocytopenia which is a disorder of the blood platelets. The platelets are cells in the blood that help with clotting. He is bleeding into his skin. That's what's causing the contusions all over his body. Since his platelet count is low we are giving him platelets intravenously and we have him on a high dosage of the steroid Prednisone."

"Can I see him?"

"Sure," said Dr. Braun as she left them and headed to the nurse's station to move on to the next patient.

Ean came into the room and walked up beside me as I laid in bed. The bed vibrated as it massaged my body.

"Hey."

"I'm such a mess."

"You're fine," said Ean trying to convince me.

"I'm sorry to put you through this."

"Don't worry."

"Take them home."

Ean left for a moment then came back with Erica and Tur.

"See you tomorrow," said Erica.

"You should go to."

"No, I want to stay."

Ean sent Erica and Tur home and stayed with me the night. The next morning I ordered him to go home.

"Go home. Tur needs you there."

"I will go later."

"No, I want you to leave. There is nothing you can do for me here."

He did not argue with me. Ean knew I was right. Besides, he was tired, and so was I. I no longer wanted to fight. The meaning my life gave to him was taking his life away.

"Go home and take care of Tur!"

Ean came over to the bed and hugged me. I could not feel him. He kissed me on the cheek.

"I love you."

He left the room.

When Ean arrived at home he walked into the living room to find Erica sitting on the sofa talking to Claudia while Tur played on the floor between them. Erica looked up at Ean with a look of concern on her face when he walked into the room. Ean never told Erica about Claudia and never brought up the situation again. Now he no longer had to because the situation had come to her. Ean headed directly for Tur and grabbed him and held him in his arms before he introduced himself. He knew who she was. She did not know him. He reacted like a mother lioness protecting her cub.

"This is Ean," said Erica.

Ean did not like the idea of having strangers in his house no less a client with a criminal history.

"Nice to meet you," said Claudia not knowing Ean was once her caseworker and responsible for her diversion to the treatment facility while she was carrying Tur.

"Did she explain Stacy's condition to you?"

"Yes, she has."

"What brings you here?"

"I wanted to meet him and see Tur."

Ean's embrace around Tur tightened when she said his name. Tur began to squirm to break himself free of the embrace. Erica got up from the sofa. Ean reached into his shirt pocket and took out an *Altoid* and gave one to Tur then placed them back in his pocket. Tur's face light up. His eyes widen when the cool sensation rushed into his mouth as he inhaled.

"C'mon let's let papa Ean talk," said Erica as she took Tur from Ean and headed outside the house.

"He looks so healthy. You are both doing a good job with him."

"It's been tough."

"Do you think it would be alright if I came to visit him sometimes?"

"I really would have to speak with Stacy about that."

"I know that I am out of line by coming here without permission first, but after you called I really wanted to know how the baby was doing."

"The agency and court require you to get permission first so that arrangements can be made."

"How is he?"

"He is holding his own. You can visit him at CVPH. We take him there since all his records have been there since the accident."

"What accident?"

"Erica didn't tell you?"

"She said he had a blood infection."

"She did not tell you how it developed?"

"No."

"Would you like a cup of tea?"

"Sure."

"Come with me," said Ean as he led Claudia into the kitchen.

She sat at the kitchen table as Ean grabbed the tea pot off the stove and filled it with water then replaced it and switched on the burner.

"Is chamomile OK?"

"Yes, thank you."

When the kettle began to whistle Ean pulled it off the stove, turned off the burner and poured them both a cup as he began to fill her in on the past five years. As he told my story Tur's laughter could be heard from outside. An hour and a half later Ean showed Claudia out.

"Thanks for everything."

"You're welcome. Do you think you will be stopping by the hospital?"

"Yeah, I'll stop by."

"I think he would like to meet you. He's in room 6B."

Ean did not know Claudia's true intentions. She originally decided to get pregnant and have Tur so that she could seek support from me. She knew from my profile at the sperm clinic that I would be a successful lawyer someday and would have adequate resources to provide for her. After talking with Ean she realized that her plans were not going to work. However, she was not convinced and had to see me for herself.

Claudia arrived at the hospital and approached the nurse's station.

"I'm looking for Room 6B."

"Right down the hall, visiting hours are almost over," said the nurse who had previously asked Ean not to return with Tur and basically threw my parents out.

"I will not be long," said Claudia as she headed for my room.

When she approached the door she was as quiet as a mouse. She stopped in the doorway and peered in. My eyelids were partly shut and I could see a hint of disgust and disappointment on her face. Erica and Ean were kind in their description of me. It did not help that she just stood there staring at my contusions and bed sores. I opened my eyes fully and startled her.

"Would you like to come in?

"I'm..."

"I know who you are. Please come in and have a seat."

"No thanks, I'll stand."

"Soot yourself"

"They didn't tell me."

"Tell you that I am a mess?"

"You are not what I expected."

"Now you know who I am."

"I want my son," said Claudia raising her voice as she rethought her plan.

She felt Tur would allow her to apply for benefits and they could collect when I was long gone, which I'm sure she calculated could not be that far off. She seemed like the type who would also force Tur to work when he got older to take care of her as she aged.

"You're a little late. You can't have Tur."

"We'll see," yelled Claudia as she turned around to leave the room and banged into the nurse who is about to throw her out.

~ ~ ~ ~

Three days later Erica was in the kitchen fixing a sandwich for Tur. There was a knock on the kitchen door. She smeared some mayonnaise over a slice of bread and completed the sandwich. Erica pulled a paper towel off a roll and wiped her hands as she answered the door. Peering out the window she smiled and opened the door.

"Hey, what are you doing up here?"

Leo walked in wearing a baseball cap and holding a small bouquet of flowers.

"I came to see you."

Leo handed her the flowers and wrapped his arms around her as Erica kissed him on his cheek.

"Give me a second. I just have to give Tur his lunch."

Erica placed the flowers on the kitchen island and pulled another towel off the roll and wrapped the sandwich in it. With sandwich in hand she went over to the refrigerator and pulled out a juice box and left the room. Leo stood in the kitchen and then took a seat at the table. Erica returned to the kitchen and sat with Leo. Leo frowned as he held his head down looking at the cap in his hand.

"Is everything alright?"

"Yeah, I just miss you."

"We talked about this. Summer break is up soon and Tur will be out of school."

"Can you get away for a couple of hours?"

"Ean is out. We can take Tur with us."

"That's OK. I want us to have time together. We've been living apart for some time now. I want you to get back to your life."

"This is my life."

"What about me? When will we be together?"

"Soon, I promise," said Erica as Leo got up from the table and headed for the door.

"Where are you going?"

"Rica! Rica!" shouted Tur from the living room.

"He's calling," said Leo as he motioned to the door that led to the living room.

"C'mon!"

"I'll see you when you get home," said Leo as he kissed her on the forehead and left.

Erica went to tend to Tur. As she headed into the living room, Ean walked through the kitchen door whistling and carrying a bag of groceries. He placed the groceries on the island and started to put them away when Erica returned to the kitchen.

"Hey I thought I saw Leo pulling out of the driveway."

"That was him."

Erica sighed.

"Are you OK?"

"He misses me."

Erica noticed red marks on Ean's neck as he reached down to put a can of beans in the cupboard.

"Where's the little runt?"

"It's nap time. He was falling asleep while eating his lunch," said Erica as she walked over to Ean and pulled on the neck of his shirt.

Ean pulled away.

"What are you doing?"

"I'm checking for Lyme disease. Stay still."

"I'm fine."

"You have some marks on your neck."

Erica realized they are love marks.

"I see."

"See?"

"You husband is being sent home to die and you are having an affair."

"It's not an affair."

"I would never cheat on Leo."

"I didn't do anything. Petting is not an affair."

"This is your way of dealing with it."

"I'm more committed than you think."

"It doesn't look like it. Stacy will be coming home tomorrow. How are you going to explain yourself?"

"There is nothing to explain."

"Then what's that on your neck? We were raised better than that."

"You don't understand."

"I know it's difficult and your hurting inside, but if you want to love, love your husband."

"Why aren't you loving you're husband?"

Erica moved closer into Ean's face.

"You want my help!"

"You don't know. You just think you do," said Ean as he folded the grocery bag and placed it in the pantry and left the kitchen.

~ ~ ~ ~

I was transported home the next day. When I arrived Ean was not there to welcome me. Erica and Tur stood by the front door of the house while the transporters brought me inside. They tried to put me in the bedroom but I argued with them to leave me in the living room. When the transporters left, Erica and Tur sat with me.

"Ean is still out shopping. He wanted to get some things before you got here."

Erica tried to cover for him. Tur would not sit still and jumped off the sofa to look for his toys.

"Would you mind making me something to eat?"

"No problem," said Erica as she got up to leave the room.

She headed for the kitchen then stopped and turned around.

"You know this is difficult for him."

"I'll have a bowl of soup," I said ignoring her statement.

I've never discussed difficulties in my relationship with her in the past and I was not about to start now. She was there for Ean, not me. Besides, I was feeling weak and wanted to save my energy.

After lunch Erica helped me into the bedroom as Tur stood beside her.

"Stand back."

"Helping papa?"

"Yes."

I felt guilty. Erica's face strained as she lifted me up out of the chair and into the bed.

"Thank you for everything."

"Not a problem."

"I know it is difficult for him but it's something we need to work out. There is a journal in the desk drawer in Tur's room. Would you please bring it to me with a pen?"

"Sure," said Erica as she left the room.

Tur stood by the bed staring at me.

"Papa Stacy loves you."

"Yes," says Tur as he smiled.

"Give papa a hug."

Tur comes over to the bed and hugs me.

"Can you remember papa loves you?" I said as Erica returned with my journal and placed it on the right side of the bed near my working arm.

"Let's let papa rest," said Erica as she reached out to Tur and led him out of the room.

"Would you mind?"

"Yes," said Erica as she turned to face me.

"Would you mind taking Tur to Albany for a few days? I would like to be alone with Ean."

"That's fine. I'll take Tur with me in the morning," said Erica as they left the room.

Ean came home the next day. He walked into the kitchen as Erica was fixing breakfast.

"Where have you been?"

"I've been trying to get my head together. You are right. This is hard to deal with."

"Don't tell me tell him."

"Is he up?"

"He requested time with you alone."

"You're leaving?"

"After breakfast I'm taking Tur with me back to Albany for a few days."

Ean left the kitchen and came into the bedroom.

"Sorry about your homecoming, I need to get myself together."

"We'll talk about it later. Help me get up for breakfast," I said as Ean helped me out of bed.

As he reached around me I noticed the love marks on his neck, so for the rest of the day I ordered him around out of anger. But then I came to the realization that I was jealous and wanted to be the only one responsible for making him feel good. I was weakening by the moment and felt myself fading away. After Erica and Tur were gone

Ean and I spent the day alone, mostly in silence. When it is time for bed I started to demand once again.

"Stay with me tonight."

I felt like I didn't have much time.

Ean looked at my journal on the nightstand beside the bed.

It was getting late and I did not have much time.

I was weak.

"Can you do one thing for me?"

"Of course I can."

"Make love to me."

"You just got out of the hospital," said Ean.

"Don't make excuses for me," I said as Ean approached and sat on the edge of the bed.

"How?"

"Take off all your clothes," I said as Ean got up from the bed and followed my directions.

Ean did as I told him. The red marks on his neck were lighter than my contusions and clearly visible. What surprised me was that Ean was physically excited. These past few years I felt so much less of a person that I did not pursue him because I believed he would not want me. But it was clear he was excited and his love tool was pointing in my direction.

"Put it in my mouth," I said as Ean climbed up on the bed.

He made love to me, stopping in between to guide my working hand over his body and reached down to rest his forehead on mine as he gently kissed my lips. Not pulling away, he did just the opposite by leaning into me. Ean did not struggle with our new found intimacy. For those moments we did not argue about how things are or how we wished them to be. We were one again. When he was done I was physically and mentally relieved because I could still give him what he needed. Ean nestled into the left side of my body and cried.

"Hey, what's wrong?"

"Nothing," said Ean.

"C'mon."

"I love you."

"You sure that was not a sympathy fuck," I said trying to lighten the moment.

"You," said Ean as he nudged into me.

"Are you going to be alright?"

"Yeah, I will. I need to tell you something."

"Don't worry. I already know."

"What?"

"The love marks on your neck."

"No, that's nothing."

"Then what?"

"I read your journal."

"I know that too. Claudia and I met at the hospital"

"I did not trust her the first time I saw her around Tur."

"You met her."

"I'm the one who sent her to you."

Ean was getting angry so I asked him to put on Artie Shaw's greatest hits to calm him down. Artie was his calming agent. Ean got up to put the CD into the alarm clock radio on the night stand and resumed his position. Ean began to fill me in on his talk with Claudia, his encounter with Mark at the pharmacy, a person he met he called the vampire, who was responsible for his love marks, and his argument with Erica. After taking it all in, I was weaker.

"Sounds like you did some crazy things in college to be accepted," said Ean as he laughed.

"We wouldn't have Tur if I didn't want. You know some things do not come from us. They are created through us. Did I ever tell you about the time I first learned about creation?"

"I don't think so," said Ean as he nestled in closer to me, and held my right hand so that I could feel him.

He waits patiently, as I told my story. I had an illumination that moment that I was just like Rona, a storyteller.

"The first philosophical discussions I ever had about creation were in kindergarten. That day in class the new letter of the day we were learning was the letter M. Ms. Green, my kindergarten teacher, taught us many words that day that began with the letter M. There was man, ironically the word moose, make believe, well that was two words but the list went on and on. During that day we drew many things that began with the letter M. The first picture I chose to draw during that lesson, Ms Green was not so impressed with, so she sat beside me to guide me."

"How did that teach you about creation?"

"Listen."

"I'm listening."

"Make a man," said Ms Green.

"But how?"

"When you draw a figure use the alphabet," she said.

"Do I use one letter to make the body?"

"You can but it's better to use a combination of letters because they make words. And words are more powerful," said Ms. Green.

"Look here. The head could be what you desire. What do you want most?"

"I want someone to play with."

"So you want a playmate? Draw a circle and put the word playmate in it. Now make the body," said Ms. Green and I drew a rectangle connected below the circle, "Why do you want a playmate?"

"To love like my mom loves me."

"Write love in the rectangle."

I drew four long jagged ellipses to symbolize the arms and legs.

"How do you wish to fill them in?" asked Ms. Green.

"In one arm I will put the word strong to help my friend and the other arm I will put the word eye to show him. These are things my mother does for me."

"Mothers provide something special," said Ms. Green as she looks at my figure.

"Do you like it?" I asked.

"Umm, I think you get the idea," said Ms. Green.

"Is this like making Frankenstein?"

"It is close but your creation is good because it comes from the heart and what comes from the heart is of God," said Ms. Green as the afternoon bell rang signaling it was time to go home.

"Did you know that a woman named Mary Shelly wrote and created Frankenstein?" asked Ms. Green.

"No."

"When you get older and read her words yourself you will understand."

Everyone in class ran to their cubicle and gathered their overcoats. Ms Green helped me clean up and put my supplies away then helped me with my overcoat. Ms Green held my hand as she led me to the door. The other children in class ran out the door of the classroom ahead of me.

"Remember the heart," Ms. Green whispered to me as she let go of my hand and I left the room carrying the figure of the man I created that day.

"So I will say the same to you. Remember the heart," I whisper to him and let go of his hand as he drifted off to sleep.

As Ean slept I reach over to the nightstand and pulled the journal to me and began to write the last events of my life and these final words to him as Artie Shaw's *Nightmare* played:

*Ean:*

*Is this the life you truly wanted? You're not alone. You're with our child Tur. How ironic. We gave the life a name and God decides to take mine away. Remember, I am always with you.*

*Love you always, Stacy.*

# Chapter VI

## Moose on the Loose

$W$hen I returned from the funeral I walked through the front door of the house and I felt its emptiness. Erica continued to take care of Tur for me. I did not come home with his ashes like we had planed. Stacy wanted to be cremated. However, that is a no-no in the Jewish tradition. Once Rona was notified of her son's death she immediately contacted a Rabbi and had his body taken away. She defied his wishes. Stacy and I spoke about it and he instructed in his will that he be cremated. When I told Rona what he wanted, she welled up in tears and went into a story of her past family members that were placed in the ovens during the Holocaust. Although I was legally married to Stacy and had all the rights to fight for his wishes, I did not want to create bad blood between Rona and myself, knowing that she is Tur's biological grandmother. With Stacy gone, I knew my life would be difficult. Raising Tur was only going to get harder. I needed all the support I could get. In my heart, I felt Rona will come around once she knew the truth about Tur.

With Stacy gone I felt like I didn't have anything. He was gone forever. My black necktie was choking me. I really wanted to pull it tighter but stopped myself and tore it off my neck then loosened the top button of my shirt and went into the bedroom. As soon as I saw the space on the bed where Stacy laid I curled up beside it and held my hand over the spot where his body slept. I pushed every thought out of my head as soon as it came in. But the most persistent thought of him broke through my defenses. Tears dripped out of my eyes and streamed down the side of my temple soaking into the pillow. The pillow absorbed my tears just as the ground took in Stacy's body an hour ago. I had to let go. Move on. What the hell was I going to do now? I asked myself. He was my guide. Stacy always knew what the right thing was for me to do. Now I had to make up my own mind and make the right decisions for Tur. When I thought of Tur the tears began to stream out of my eyes again. I wanted this life as long as Stacy was with me. Stacy decided my life for me. The moment he was hurt and could not live the life we dream about, the fairy tale was over. I wanted my life to be over and started to plan its ending when my cell phone rang. I wiped my face and reached for the phone.

"Hello."

"Hi, this is Mark. We met in the pharmacy."

"Yeah,"

"Is this a bad time?"

"I just got back from a funeral."

"Was it your friend you mentioned?"

"Yes."

"I'm sorry to hear. I was calling to see if you wanted to get together."

"It's too soon."

"Maybe we can get together some other time?"

"Thanks for understanding," I said and shut my cell phone off.

After Mark's called I closed my eyes and fell asleep.

For the next few days I laid in bed only to get up to use the bathroom and eat a few crackers when my stomach began to ache from hunger. The phone rang constantly but I didn't get up to answer it. I did not want to be bothered. What I did know was that I didn't want to live. I felt like I had nothing without him. Life had no meaning. I walked through the house looking around. When I looked outside the kitchen door I noticed the mailbox overflowing with mail, so I went outside and grabbed the mail out of the box. As I crawled back in bed with the mail in hand I could smell the scent of my body. My underarms smelled pungent but it was not as strong as the smell that rose from my bottom. It was an odor of homelessness. I was half way there. Both Tur and I would be on the street if I did not pay the bills. Stacy left a substantial insurance policy behind. He always made sure the bills were paid. I was only responsible for one credit card bill that I used to charge whatever I want.

As I sifted through the mail I noticed a letter from the adoption agency with Jeanine's name on the return address label. I opened the letter and read. Jeanine wrote that the agency was in the process of reviewing Tur's adoption. The agency received an application from Claudia to regain all parental rights and guardianship. A hearing was scheduled in two weeks. A correspondence copy was sent to Lavonda. My face became warm and the veins in the back on my neck pulsed. I really was not surprised. Stacy had expected this, but now I was left to handle it. I reached over to the nightstand and picked up the phone to call Lavonda.

"Hi, it's Ean."

"Do you know what time it is?"

"Yes."

"What's going on?"

"Did you get the letter from Jeanine? Tur's biological mother is trying to get custody of him."

"No, what does the letter say?"

I read the letter to Lavonda.

"I'm on trial now but I can come up on Sunday."

"She came to see us before Stacy passed."

"We'll talk on Sunday."

"Thank you for coming to the funeral."

"No need for that. See you then," she said and hung up the phone.

My head was killing me. I got up from the bed and went in to the bathroom. I opened the cabinet above the sink and looked through it for some aspirin. Stacy always had tons of the stuff and Tums for his heartburn. There was also the bottle of *Ambien* Dr. Braun prescribed to help me sleep after the accident. I took 500mg of aspirin and undressed. I reached over to get a razor and shaving cream.

Cut your wrist.

I shaved.

After my shave I took a hot shower. I just sat on Stacy's shower stool and let the water cascade over my body. I laid in his spot on the bed, now I was sitting where he sat when he showered and began to cry. My want for him hurt. I continued to push thoughts out of my head as they entered.

Take the pills.

I have to get out.

Drown yourself.

I have to get out.

I stood up from the chair and turned the water off. After drying off I dressed in a pair of jeans and a crisp white tee-shirt. In desperation I called Erica.

"Hello."

"What time is it?"

"Who is that?" asked Leo in the background.

"It's early."

"It's my brother."

"I'm coming to see Tur today," I said.

"Are you ready for us to come back?"

"What's wrong with him, doesn't he know what time it is?" asked Leo.

"Yeah, can you come up Sunday?" I asked.

"When is he going to come and take care of his own kid?" asked Leo.

"Shush!"

"Hello."

"I'll see you later," I said as Erica hung up the phone.

"Go back to bed," said Erica.

"I'm up now," said Leo.

"Why do you have to enable him?"

"He is in a vulnerable state."

"He has to grow up at some point. Don't you think?"

"Will you go back to bed!"

"You can't take care of him all his life."

"He just lost Stacy."

"I know. I know, but your emotional bond is incestuous," said Leo as he pulled the covers back and got out of bed and left the room, Erica explained to me when she came up that Sunday.

My extreme anxiety grew more intense, so I called Rona.

"It's Ean, Stacy's spouse."

"It's quite early dear. Is everything alright?"

"Yes, I need to speak with you. Is it alright if I drop by today?"

"Today we have golf."

"I really need to speak with you about Stacy."

"Please stop by around noon."

"See you then," I said and hung up the phone.

My thoughts were coming to me rapidly. It was a six hour drive to Westchester. I needed to get out and arrived at noon as Rona suggested.

Rona sat me down in her sun room for tea and biscuits. We could see Stacy's father in the back yard practicing his golf swing.

"You have a very nice home," I said.

Stacy never brought me here. He knew I was not truly welcome.

"What is it you needed to talk to me about?"

"It's about Stacy and Tur."

"What about them?"

"Tur is Stacy's biological child."

"What are you saying?"

"Tur is your grandchild."

"And how is that?"

"It's a long story but I really came here because I need your help."

"Tell me how that it is I have a grandchild?"

I went into the story of how Stacy donated sperm when he was in college that resulted in Tur's birth, and how Claudia fit in.

"Why didn't he tell us?"

"I don't know."

"So what can we do now?"

"Claudia is trying to get custody of him and I need your help to keep him."

"Isn't that for a judge to decide?"

"Yes, but I need your support on this."

"I don't know what difference it would make."

"You're his biological grandmother and could apply to become his full guardian or have say in who should care for him."

"I'm too old to care for a child."

"I'm asking for your help so that Claudia does not get custody."

"I'm sorry but I really don't think I can. My son was my only family."

I wanted to question her about Stacy's sister but let it go.

"Thanks for seeing me," I said and then got up to leave.

As I was leaving Rona got up and came after me.

"Are you sure that is my grandchild?"

I stopped and turned to her.

"Yes," I said and walked out of the house.

I drove back to Mooers stopping by at Erica's. When I arrived she is in her studio showing Tur how to use finger paints. I walked in and when Tur saw me he shouted.

"Papa Ean!"

He learned to pronounce my name correctly. I kissed him as he reached up to me and smeared watercolors all over my shirt as he hugged me. Erica also hugged me.

"I just wanted to see how you were doing."

"I thought you wanted us to come up Sunday?"

"Just in the neighborhood so I thought I would stop by."

"Would you like something to eat?"

"No thanks."

"Are you sure you're alright? You don't look well."

"I'm fine. I'll see you on Sunday," I said as I headed for the door.

"Where are you going? You just got here."

"I feel like I have to keep moving."

"You got to get it together. I don't know if I can help out any longer."

"Why not?"

"Leo is talking about separating. I don't want to lose him."

"I have a meeting with Lavonda next week. Claudia is trying to have the adoption revoked and get full custody of Tur."

"I'll bring him back up Sunday."

"Leo will come around."

"I hope so."

"Is everything alright? You seem energized. You're not drugging are you?"

"No."

"Your speech is so quick."

"I'm fine. I got to go."

"You don't look fine," said Erica as I kissed Tur on the forehead and left.

I drove around till I ended up at the Raw Hide where I had met the "Vampire" who sucked on my neck when I was away. The bar was empty with the exception of the bartender who was wiping down the counter as he watched the local news on a television that hung over the corner of the bar.

"Would you mind making me a gin and tonic?"

"That's what I'm here for."

"Getting an early start?"

Mind your fucking business. I came to drink not to talk, I thought. He brought me my drink in a chilled glass. I was still burning up inside over that bitch Claudia who was making my life more difficult. Wasn't it enough that I lost Stacy? A part of me was relieved that I did not have to clean up after his shit, but I want him with me. Life was bittersweet. After the first three drinks I chugged down in less than ten minutes I was feeling better. I just leaned on the edge of the stool and stared at the television. The bartender turned to me.

"Another?"

"Yeah."

He poured another and slid it across the top of the counter to me. A few people started to trickle in. They were mostly much older gay couples.

"Hi," said one of the couples who took a seat beside me.

I ignore them, grabbed my drink, got up and headed over to a chair in the dark corner of the room beside a speaker so that I could drown in the music. Later on that night I went to use the bathroom and when I returned the Vampire was sitting in the chair beside mine. When I sat down he leaned over and shouted at me.

"How are you?"

"Not tonight!" I shouted back.

He turned away wounded. He did not recognize me or the faint marks on my neck that he had caused a few weeks back. At eleven thirty Mark walked into the bar with two other guys. He did not see me in the dark corner through the crowd that gathered on the small dance floor as he scanned the room. Mark got up to use the restroom after finishing his first drink. When he returned to the bar I got up from the chair and approached the edge of the bar to order another drink. The bartender saw me and approached.

"Make it a large."

"Are you OK?"

"I'm fine."

Mark looked over to me but I did not acknowledge him. I took the drink from the bartender and swaggered out of the bar sipping the drink. I had a difficult time remembering where I had parked but then remembered the car was in the second spot by the entrance. I swayed back and forth as I moved closer to my vehicle and placed my drink on the hood of the car when I got to it. As I reached into my pocket for my keys the music from the bar got louder then muffled as patrons walk in and out. Everything was clouded. As I struggled to pull my keys out of my pocket Mark grabbed my hand.

"Let me help you," said Mark as he reached in and pulled out my keys.

"I'm alright," I said.

"You can't drive in your condition."

I struggled with him for the keys. I let go when I realize his grip was stronger than mine.

"OK."

"I'll drive you home. Where do you live?" he asked as he put the key in the door and opened the car.

"I live off State Street in Mooers."

"Do you need this?" asked Mark as he took my drink off the hood of the car.

"Yes, it helps with the pain."

Mark poured the drink out on the ground and handed the empty plastic cup to me. I took the cup and went around the car to the passengers' side. Mark started the car and waited patiently for me to get in. Mark turned to me when I got in the car.

"I thought it was too soon?"

"You don't understand."

"Then help me."

I remained silent until we got to State Street.

"There, the second house on the left. No, the third house on the right."

"Which is it?"

"There, the one on the right."

Mark parked in the driveway and helped me out of the car. He walked me to the door and searched for the house key. Mark tried a few before he found the right one and opened the door. He lead me to the living room and sat me on the sofa. Mark took the car key off my key ring.

"I need to borrow your car to get home."

"Take it, but promise you will bring it back."

133

"I promise. Besides you have my name and number."

I sat on the edge of the sofa staring into space. My body was numb but my head was spinning.

"I better get going. Are you going to be alright?"

"I will be, after I throw up."

Mark helped me to the bathroom and held me over the toilet. I puked three times. It was all liquid. He returned me to the couch then left. After he left I go back up to use the bathroom again. After relieving myself I opened the bathroom cabinet for some aspirin and inadvertently grabbed the bottle of *Ambien* and went into the bedroom.

~ ~ ~ ~

The next day there was a persistent knock on the front door. I was too weak to answer it, but I mustered enough energy to pull myself out of bed. When I opened the door Rona bolted in carrying a small bag.

"Where is my grandchild?"

She looked around the kitchen and headed into the living room.

"There is no one else here!" I said holding the front door open.

After my meeting with her I decided she was not welcome.

"Tur!" she called.

"There is nobody else here!" I shouted over her.

Stacy's father was sitting in their black Lincoln Town Car in the driveway.

Rona came back into the kitchen.

"Where is he?"

"My sister has him."

"I brought this for him," said Rona as she handed me a small *Tiffany* shopping bag.

"Thank you," I said not knowing what it was.

"Teach the child the canon," said Rona as she walked out the door to leave.

Rona walked off the porch then stopped and came back to the door.

"Thank you for telling me the truth."

"I felt you should know."

She nodded her head, turned around and walked off the porch. I watched her as Stacy's father opened the door for her. She hopped in the car and they drove off. Holding the bag in one hand I closed the door with my foot and sat down at the kitchen table. I was curious as to what Rona brought for Tur. I opened the bag wide and peered into it. At first I thought she bought Tur some engraved Tiffany's blocks wrapped in string but I reached in and pulled out two 40mm Tefillin. I first heard about phylacteries from Stacy. In the bag there was a ShelRosh for the head and a ShelYad for the arm. The only reason I knew what they were is because Stacy gave me the proper education of a boy in a Yeshiva. He taught me how to read the Hebrew language and that the boxes held the biblical teaching that established the covenant with God. The covenant is that one will dedicate oneself to God in whatever one does. I placed the boxes on the table and threw the bag on the floor. Stacy's mother was out of her mind. Tur was only five. Tradition dictates that a child should not use Tefillin until after their thirteenth birthday. A woman of her tradition should have known that a dreidel was more appropriate. I

looked down at the objects in front of me and
began to separate the SheRosh to get at its
contents. Stacy taught me that each box held the
four verses of the Torah that tells the
commandments of the Tefillin. When I opened the
box there were two small scrolls of parchment. I
took one out and unravel it. The paper was so
brittle. The paper was almost the size of a fortune
in a Chinese cookie. I read to myself the
parchment of Deuteronomy 6:4-8:

ד שְׁמַע, יִשְׂרָאֵל: יְהוָה אֱלֹהֵינוּ, יְהוָה
אֶחָד.
ה וְאָהַבְתָּ, אֵת יְהוָה אֱלֹהֶיךָ, בְּכָל-לְבָבְךָ
וּבְכָל-נַפְשְׁךָ, וּבְכָל-מְאֹדֶךָ.
ו וְהָיוּ הַדְּבָרִים הָאֵלֶּה, אֲשֶׁר אָנֹכִי מְצַוְּךָ
הַיּוֹם--עַל-לְבָבֶךָ.
ז וְשִׁנַּנְתָּם לְבָנֶיךָ, וְדִבַּרְתָּ בָּם, בְּשִׁבְתְּךָ
בְּבֵיתֶךָ וּבְלֶכְתְּךָ בַדֶּרֶךְ, וּבְשָׁכְבְּךָ וּבְקוּמֶךָ.
ח וּקְשַׁרְתָּם לְאוֹת, עַל-יָדֶךָ; וְהָיוּ לְטֹטָפֹת,
בֵּין עֵינֶיךָ.*

I stopped reading and realized what she meant
by teach the child the canon. I rolled the
parchment back up and placed it in the box. I got
up from the table and headed back into the

---

* *"Hear; O Israel the Lord is our God, The Lord is
One and you shall love the Lord your God, with all
your heart, with all your soul, and with all your
means. And these words which I command you
this day shall be upon your heart. And you shall
teach them to your children..."*

bedroom. The phone rang and I ignored it. The answering machine picked up and I could hear Erica leaving a message.

"It's me. I'm just checking on you. Tur wants to say hi. He has been asking for his papa," said Erica as the machine cut her off.

Mark came back that afternoon to return the car as promised. I was a bit groggy from the pills I took. Mark came in and sat at the kitchen table. He looked at the bag on the floor and the Tefillin on the table.

"Let me get that out of your way."

I grabbed the phylacteries off the table and picked up the bag from the floor. Mark watched me as I placed the phylacteries in the bag. I carried the bag into the bedroom and place it on the nightstand then returned.

"Would you like to go out for lunch? I know a great place."

"Is it lunch time already."

My stomach is killing me. The pills ate at my stomach. Mark looked at his watch.

"It's 12:15pm."

"Give me a second," I said and went into the bathroom to straighten my hair and brush my teeth.

After brushing I splashed water on my face and smiled in the mirror. It was like lifting cement. My cheeks dropped as soon as I let go of the muscles in my face. I didn't bother to shower or change my clothes. I reeked of the bar. Mark sat patiently. When I entered he smiled at me.

"Ready?"

"Let's go."

"I filled up the tank. I just ask that you return the favor and drop me off after lunch."

"I can do that," I said as we got into the car and drove off.

The first thing I noticed about being with Mark was that I felt comfortable behind the wheel as we drove to the café. Although hung over I felt at ease and thought it was because I was being treated as if I had permission. He did a better job of providing directions than I did the night before. We reach *Moose on the Loose Café*. There he ordered us two lunch specials of turkey clubs and toped it off with *Moose Tracks* ice cream for dessert.

While eating I filled Mark in on the last five years of my life.

"It sounds like it was difficult taking care of him and the baby."

"I've been carrying around this guilt because part of me wished that he died so that I would not have to deal with it."

"When you say "it" do you mean the situation or Tur?"

I hesitated for a moment and realized how perceptive of my subconscious he was.

"I guess the situation," I said not being truly honest.

"Well, you're no longer in the situation."

"Yeah, but I don't want the life that I have now."

"Why don't you?"

"Stacy was everything for me. He took care of everything."

"You don't believe you are a masculine image of a female, do you? A Geisha Moose?"

"Geisha Moose?"

"Sorry, I'm a moose man."

I paused and thought about the moose head that was mounted to the wall in Tur's room.

"What do you think about taxidermy?"

"Why are you asking?"

"Just curious."

"Well if the animal was not killed for the trophy then I guess it is alright. Some people have it done to their pets so that they will have them around after the pet dies. Museums do it. Why are you curious?"

"I've inherited a stuffed moose. I will have to show you some time."

"A full moose?"

"No just the head."

"I'll be happy to see it. We were talking about Stacy. Was Stacy the male hero in your relationship? Was he the majestic lord of the manner?"

"It felt like it."

"Listen, that idea is a social construct adopted by humans."

"Worn like a jacket?"

"Exactly, listen I know moose and it's a false belief that male bulls are dominant. Most bulls die during the rut from malnutrition. Why? Because the female cows hardly pay attention to the aggressive displays and push the male bull away until it's ready to mate. It is the female who is in control. Even if the male bull gets aggressive and tries to take what he wants the female is stronger to fight him off. The female cows stay in herds and protect the group. The individual male bull stays in solitude throughout the rut, roaming and psychotically lovesick until the female is ready. The majestic antlers that flourish on the male bull during the rut weigh him down and make him vulnerable to disease and predators."

"What does that have to do with me and Stacy?"

"Who was the one in control in your relationship? I bet you called the shots when it came to the lovemaking. Remember it is "she" who is in control and calls when ready."

I thought about Mark's words then smiled at him in silence as I remembered reading the story Stacy wrote in his journal that he left behind for Tur. He was the bull and I was the cow.

"Tell me more?" I asked.

Mark lifted my spirits.

"Maybe another time, I have to get to work."

It was not until I dropped Mark off at the DEC that I realized that it was he who called me about the moose when Stacy was in the hospital. As he climbed out of the car I reached over and pulled him back in.

"It was you who was assigned to track the moose that caused the accident."

"Yes."

"Why didn't you say anything when I told you my life story?"

"I didn't want to interrupt."

I looked at Mark in wonder.

"Would you like to come with me on my adventure weekend?"

I was intrigued.

"Sure what do you have in mind?"

"It will be a surprise."

"I'll pick you up at 10:00am next Saturday," said Mark as he climbed out of the car and headed for his office.

When I got home I went straight into the bathroom. My stomach was cramped from the food since I had only eaten a few crackers the past week and took pills on an empty stomach. I used the bathroom then went back into the bedroom to pick up Stacy's journal from the nightstand, slid myself out of my sneakers and laid on the bed. That morning I woke up beside him. He still had the pen in his hand. I remembered pulling it from his cold fingers. His face was pale and his lips were blue. One look at him and I knew he was gone. My life started to change that evening while I sat on the bed and picked up his journal and began to read where I left off: "*When I entered the room Ean was snoring...*" Was this a dream? It could not have been for Stacy would then have walked over to the side of the bed, lifted himself out of his slippers and slid onto the bed beside me. I would then have spooned his body and exchanged an "I love you" as he fell asleep.

~ ~ ~ ~

The next day I woke up really early again. Stacy used to call me an early riser. It was three o'clock in the morning. When I screened clients for depression, I knew that waking up hours earlier than normal was a sign of depression. I had suicidal ideation, stopped eating and showering. What's happening to me? Am I dead? I can't be. To prove this to myself I got up out of the bed, shaved, took a shower and got dressed. It sounded like this all happened at once but it took me a while to get myself together. Thoughts of Stacy continued to dominate my mind. As I thought of Stacy and what he wrote, it propelled me to go into Tur's room and sit at the desk and begin to write where Stacy left off. My first line "*When I returned from the funeral I walked through the front door of the house and I felt its emptiness,*" reflected how I felt. After that first line I stopped writing and got up from the desk and went back into the bedroom and looked at the bottle of pills that were on the night stand. The bottle of *Ambien* was still full. I went into the kitchen to fix a pot of coffee. Just as the coffee machine finished Mark came by to pick me up. He was early. I poured a cup.

"Would you like some?"

"No thanks, we should get going."

Mark radiated cheer. He had so much energy from the time he walked through the door. Mark tried to wrap his arms around me, but I pulled away. It felt good to be held for that moment. My mind shifted to darker thoughts the moment he let go.

"Are you ready?"

"Let me finish my coffee."

He stayed watching me as I chugged the coffee down.

"Let's go."

"Where are we going?"

"It's a surprise," said Mark as we got in his car and drove.

"Did you eat anything?"

"No."

"We should have a light breakfast," said Mark as he drove into the parking lot of the local *Dunkin Donuts*.

We grabbed a bagel and got back in the car. Mark drove along I-87 until we reached the exit for the Plattsburgh International Airport.

"Where are you taking me?"

"To the sky," said Mark as he smiled at me then focused on the road that led into the airport.

Mark turned off a smaller road that led to the airport's back entrance. As we entered the airport there was a sign on the gate that read Plattsburgh Flight School.

"You're not going to teach me how to fly a plane, are you?"

"No, but I will teach you how to fly without one," said Mark as he pulled the car up to the flight school.

Outside was a sign posted for skydiving lessons.

"Don't tell me we're going skydiving?"

"Precisely!" said Mark grinning.

"I am afraid of heights."

"You'll get over it."

Mark parked the car.

"I'll wait here and watch," I said as we got out of the car.

"C'mon."

Mark walked around the car and grabbed me by the arm and led me into the office.

"Hey guys, going up today?" asked the flight instructor.

"It's just the two of us."

"We're airborne in forty-five minutes. Go get your gear."

Mark wrapped his arm around my shoulders and led me into the hanger. There was a rack that held body suits and parachutes that were

143

inspected and packed earlier that morning. The flight instructor came in behind us.

"What's your size?"

"I'm a medium."

"Is this your first time?"

"Yeah," I said as beads of sweat formed on my forehead.

"We'll give instructions in ten minutes."

"Do you have a bathroom?"

"Over in the corner."

"Don't worry, you will be fine," said Mark as I made a bee line for the bathroom.

In the bathroom I splashed water on my face and ripped a towel from the dispenser to dry off. I stood staring in the mirror trying to convince myself that everything was fine and that I was there for a reason. When I returned to Mark the fear disappeared. My thoughts started to come more quickly. Life started to make sense to me. I believed that I met Mark for a reason. Jumping out of a plane at thirty-five thousand feet was now making sense. As I tried on a jumpsuit I noticed a poster on the wall beside me that read "Skydying". My heart started to pound harder and I could physically feel my pupils dilate then contract. I blinked my eyes and refocused on the flyer with the man jumping out of the plane. The words on the poster read Skydiving. My underarms were sweaty. Mark came over and explained the type of gear that was used and told me how to exit the plane and land once we reached the ground. As he was explaining the instructor called us over with two other couples scheduled to take the plunge. The instructor guided us through the preparation phase. As he instructed, Mark harnessed me into the straps that were attached to his shoot mounted on his back. We practiced jumping out and landing.

"While in the air keep this form," said the instructor.

"There is nothing to it," said Mark.

"OK."

"Are you ready?" asked Mark.

The plane arrived at the entrance to take us up. One of the women of the couples turned to me.

"We are on our honeymoon and thought this would be memorable."

"Congratulations!" I said.

At that moment I began to struggle with memories of life with Stacy and felt a sense of clarity come over me, believing Mark was my gateway to Stacy. Mark had unharnessed me so that we could climb into the plane. When we boarded, the wife of the honeymooners began to chat endlessly. It was obvious nervous chatter. I, on the other hand, responded just the opposite. Silence overcame me. As the plane ascended into the sky the flight instructor directed us to prepare for the jump. I climbed back into the harness. Mark tightened the straps and clamped the metal supports hooking us together. The instructor double checked our gear and we all sat waiting for the moment.

"Are you ready?"

"I better be," I said to Mark as he blew in my ear.

"That is what it will sound like."

When the plane reached the right altitude the instructor then motioned to us to line up. He slid open the plane door. One by one each couple approached the door with their guide. The instructor gave them one quick look over as they position themselves at the door. When it is our turn Mark held on to the edge of the door while I dangled out the door of the plane. My instinct was to look down. Mark grabbed my head and pulled it back towards his chest then rocked back to the count of three as we practiced on the ground, and jumped. My heart raced as I initially gasped for air. Once I relaxed into Mark's body and went with the flow I gave in to the pull of gravity. The sky was a crystal blue on the horizon. A ray of sunshine beamed across the sky. This was nirvana. I decided this is how I wanted my life to end.

I began to unclip the metal clasps that connected me to Mark. In my mind I could clearly see the picture of Da Vinci's *Studies of Embryos* on the cover of Stacy's journal and started to pull at the straps of the harness. I wanted to sever the umbilical cord that held my connection to life.

"What the hell are you doing?"

Mark grabbed onto my wrist to keep the formation then realized what I was doing. Because of my sharp movements we were losing formation and beginning to descend rapidly as I kicked my feet.

"Stop!" Mark screamed.

Mark was losing control as we both accelerated to the ground. Mark quickly pulled the parachute chord and our bodies went flying in the reverse direction. We were sucked back up into the sky as the parachute opened. I stopped tugging and inhaled as we were thrown back up into the sky. Mark held the handles of the

146

parachute chords as he put pressure on my upper arm trying to prevent me from detaching myself. Even if I got the upper straps loose I realized that I would have to flip my body over to get my legs out of the harness. My goal was to end my life, not Mark's.

The parachute glided as Mark squeezed my upper chest area trying to gain control. When we got closer to the ground Mark loosened his embrace and tugged on the cord handles to lift us slightly as our feet hit the ground. The parachute fell to the ground and pulled us to the left. Mark grabbed my body and held me tight to prevent the parachute from dragging us.

"What are you thinking? You almost got us killed."

I did not respond. My vision was clear. Mark unhooked me from his harness and I walked to the office as he gathered the parachute. I took off the skydiving gear. Mark looked back at me as I dropped the gear on the ground and headed to the car to wait for him. I sat in the car and waited for Mark to drive me home. Mark exited the hanger and picked up my gear to return it. When he is done he came to the car. He opened the door and sat in the driver's seat. He was silent for a moment then turned to me.

"What is wrong with you?"

No response.

"I'm asking you a question."

No response.

Mark took a deep breath and let it out. He turned on the ignition and drove out of the airport. I remained silent for the whole ride. My mind was not right. When Mark pulled into my driveway I remained still in the passenger's seat.

"Well?"

Dead silence. We sat there for a few moments.

"Listen I really like you but I need stability. I can't be with someone who wants to off themselves."

No longer wanting to hear Mark preach to me, I opened the door to leave the vehicle.

"He's gone! Get over it and get out of the rut you're in!" he shouted at me as I left the vehicle.

Mark watched me as I walked up the porch steps and grabbed the mail before I entered, not looking back. When I shut the door I could hear his car pull out of the driveway.

# Chapter VII

## Running with the Bulls

The following day I was expecting Lavonda at the house to talk with me about both petitions filed for custody of Tur. When I checked the mail after Mark dropped me off the previous Sunday, there was another letter from Jeanine stating that Rona was also seeking custody of Tur. The fact that both Claudia and Rona wanted Tur put me way over the edge. The rest of the weekend I stayed in bed. With Stacy gone, I had a strong mental block and a form of learned helplessness. There was going to be a joint hearing before Judge Lamb. I had to pull myself together. Obviously I was lonely, but I thought it was too soon to have someone else in my life. Besides, I did not know if Mark wanted to see me again let alone how he would take to Tur and vice-versa. I was assured he would not have a problem with the moose head mounted to the wall in Tur's room. But I still had to make peace with *l'orignal*. More basically, I did not know if I could take care of Tur on my own, knowing Erica would not be able to put her life on hold any longer. Leo has had enough. Lavonda knocked on the front door. At 9:00am I pulled myself out of bed to let her in. When I opened the door she took one look at me and was not kind.

"You look like hell."

"I'm just trying to keep it together."

"I think you need to try a little harder."

"It's nice to see you too," I said as we went into the living room.

"I have to be upfront with you. We are in for a tough fight."

"I am Tur's legal parent. I am legally married to Stacy and have adopted his biological child."

"Are you alright?"

"I'm fine."

"Then what biological child nonsense are you talking about."

"I'm not talking nonsense. Tur is Stacy's biological child."

"How is that?"

I explained to Lavonda how Claudia's anonymous sperm donor was Stacy.

"So he knew this when he asked me to represent you guys?"

"Don't feel so betrayed. I was in the dark until recently."

"We have to subpoena the records from the sperm bank."

"There is plenty of DNA evidence here to prove a match."

"This case could set a precedent."

"Only if we win."

"I will need copies of Claudia's non-compliance records from T.A.S.C. to help discredit her. Rona is going to be much more difficult."

"Would it help our case that she is non-maternal, and a religious fanatic who expressed to me that she is too old to take care of a child?"

"Has she had any involvement with him?"

"Not at all, but she did drop off a bizarre inappropriate gift for him."

"What was it?"

"She dropped off religious paraphernalia."

Lavonda looked at me confused.

"Jewish prayer boxes."

"Oh, OK. We'll have to work on that part of the case. I have to get going," said Lavonda as she got up to leave.

I walked her to the door. Before she left she gave me a hug and some advice.

"Please shave for the court hearing."

"Don't worry I will."

"Take care of yourself. Stacy would not want to see you like this," said Lavonda.

It was 10:15am when Lavonda left. As soon as I closed the door behind her I jetted for the bathroom to wash up. I hoped in the car to head to Albany but before I left I sat in the driveway to get my mind together. My goal was to build a case against Claudia as soon as possible. The thought of going back to my old job made my body tremble. Not only did I leave them high and dry during a busy time of the year, but I did not know how they would take to me if I walked through the front door, so I pulled out my cell phone and called Saudi.

"Mr. Ean how are you?" she whispered to me.

"Listen, I need your help."

"What's going on?"

"I need you to get me a copy of Claudia Braunstein's file."

"You know I'm not supposed to do that."

"I really need your help."

"Why do you need it?"

"Claudia is trying to take Tur away from me."

"What does that have to do with the file?"

"We have to prove to the judge that she will be an unfit mother."

"I don't think you want to come by here. They're still upset that you left. I'll fax you the file."

"Are you sure?"

"I'll camouflage it as a referral."

"Please call me if there is anything new with her case."

I gave Saudi the fax number to the Rite Aid where I met Mark and drove over to retrieve it.

Erica's Explorer was in the driveway when I got back to the house with fax in hand. As soon as I walked through the door Tur came charging at me.

"Ean!"

He wrapped his arms around my hips. I reached down to lift him up into my arms and place the fax on the counter. Erica was sitting on the sofa when I entered the living room. As I carried Tur into the room Erica got up from the sofa and walked towards us.

"I have to get going."

"You're not staying?"

"I just came to drop him off," said Erica as she reached up to kiss Tur on the cheek then me.

"I'm not ready for him."

"No parent is ever ready," she said as she headed for the door.

I followed her out of the house to the Explorer, still carrying Tur.

"Please, things are not quite right yet!"

"I have to get back to my life. It's about time."

"Please!"

Erica's face grew red and tears welled up in her eyes as she got into her car and drove off.

"Erica!" shouted Tur.

I stood in the driveway as Tur began to cry.

"Erica! Erica!"

As he cried I carried him back into the house and placed him on the floor and lead him by hand into his room. Tur continued to cry as the phone rang. I placed him in his bed with a blanket over him and left to answer the phone.

"It's Mark."

"Hi."

"I'm just calling to let you know that we caught the male bull that was responsible for Stacy's accident."

"Why are you telling me this?"

"Is everything alright?"

"Sorry, it's just that I'm in a difficult situation."

"Is it something I can help out with?"

"It involves someone else you haven't met."

"Well it appears the bull was running rabid because of a parasite we call brain worm. The

153

parasite affects a moose's nervous system and can ultimately result in death. We are treating it, but the infection may be too advanced. You are still entitled to the carcass."

"I thought you were trying to save it?"

"We might have to euthanize it."

"No, thank you."

"Let me know if you change your mind?"

"Wait! I want to be there if you put it down."

"OK."

"Mark. I'm sorry about what happened yesterday. Can we start over?"

"Sorry, but I just called to tell you about the bull."

"Oh."

"I'll call you soon," said Mark as he hung up the phone.

Tur's cries diminished to a soft whine. I peeked in on him. He was curled up in a ball drifting off to sleep. I turned around and went into the bedroom and sat on the bed and stared into space. I began to smell the scent of leather and looked over at the *Tiffany* bag. The Tefillin that I had opened was in the bag on the nightstand. I grabbed the bag knocking over the bottle of *Ambien*. I held the bag in one hand as I picked up the bottle of *Ambien* in the other and sat it upright on the table. I emptied the Tefillin on my lap and tossed the bag to the floor. With my index finger nail I began to tear open the box and pulled out the scrolls I hadn't read. I read the commandments of Deuteronomy 11:12-14:

יב אֶרֶץ, אֲשֶׁר-יְהוָה אֱלֹהֶיךָ דֹּרֵשׁ אֹתָהּ:
תָּמִיד, עֵינֵי יְהוָה אֱלֹהֶיךָ בָּהּ--מֵרֵשִׁית הַשָּׁנָה,
וְעַד אַחֲרִית שָׁנָה. {ס}
יג וְהָיָה, אִם-שָׁמֹעַ תִּשְׁמְעוּ אֶל-מִצְוֹתַי, אֲשֶׁר
אָנֹכִי מְצַוֶּה אֶתְכֶם, הַיּוֹם--לְאַהֲבָה אֶת-יְהוָה
אֱלֹהֵיכֶם, וּלְעָבְדוֹ, בְּכָל-
לְבַבְכֶם, וּבְכָל-נַפְשְׁכֶם.
-עמש ועמשת לא-מיתוצ רשא יכנא הוצמ
יד וְנָתַתִּי מְטַר-אַרְצְכֶם בְּעִתּוֹ, יוֹרֶה
וּמַלְקוֹשׁ; וְאָסַפְתָּ דְגָנֶךָ, וְתִירֹשְׁךָ וְיִצְהָרֶךָ.†

The words lifted off the page and pulsed in
three dimensions towards my eyes. Large pellets
of rain fell from the sky and bounced off the
window. Early evenings like this Stacy and I
would stay snuggled together in bed until the sun
broke through and the sky cleared. The sky
cracked as thunder roared and lightning shot
through the sky. I could see the windows light up
for a few seconds then darken. I opened up the
next scroll and continued to read Exodus 13:1-6:

א וַיְדַבֵּר יְהוָה, אֶל-מֹשֶׁה לֵּאמֹר.

---

† *"And it shall come to pass, if ye shall hearken
diligently unto My Commandments which I
command you this day, to love the LORD your
God, and to serve Him with all your heart and with
all your soul, that I will give the rain of your land
in its season, the former rain and the latter rain,
that thou mayest gather in thy corn, and thy wine,
and thine oil…,"*

155

ב  קַדֶּשׁ-לִי כָל-בְּכוֹר פֶּטֶר כָּל-רֶחֶם, בִּבְנֵי
יִשְׂרָאֵל--בָּאָדָם, וּבַבְּהֵמָה:  לִי, הוּא.
ג  וַיֹּאמֶר מֹשֶׁה אֶל-הָעָם, זָכוֹר אֶת-הַיּוֹם
הַזֶּה אֲשֶׁר יְצָאתֶם מִמִּצְרַיִם מִבֵּית עֲבָדִים, כִּי
בְּחֹזֶק יָד, הוֹצִיא יְהוָה אֶתְכֶם מִזֶּה; וְלֹא יֵאָכֵל,
חָמֵץ.
ד  הַיּוֹם, אַתֶּם יֹצְאִים, בְּחֹדֶשׁ, הָאָבִיב.
ה  וְהָיָה כִי-יְבִיאֲךָ יְהוָה אֶל-אֶרֶץ הַכְּנַעֲנִי
וְהַחִתִּי וְהָאֱמֹרִי וְהַחִוִּי וְהַיְבוּסִי, אֲשֶׁר נִשְׁבַּע
לַאֲבֹתֶיךָ לָתֶת לָךְ, אֶרֶץ זָבַת חָלָב, וּדְבָשׁ;
וְעָבַדְתָּ אֶת-הָעֲבֹדָה הַזֹּאת, בַּחֹדֶשׁ הַזֶּה.
ו  שִׁבְעַת יָמִים, תֹּאכַל מַצֹּת; וּבַיּוֹם,
הַשְּׁבִיעִי, חַג, לַיהוָה.‡

The words continued to lift up off the paper
and jump out at me. I could feel my eyeballs
pulse. Lightning flashed outside the window and a
loud crackling noise turned to a loud roar that
echoed through the house. Tur screamed from his
room. I jumped off the bed and ran to him. When I
entered the room he was still asleep. I scooped
him up in my arms, blanket and all, and carry him
back to my room. The walk to the room seemed
like a long journey. I laid him on the bed. My
head felt cloudy but my thoughts were fiery. Tur

---

‡ *"And the LORD spoke unto Moses, saying:
'Sanctify unto Me all the first-born, whatsoever
openeth the womb among the children of Israel,
both of man and of beast, it is Mine.'..."*

opened his eyes when I sat on the bed and looked up at me.

"Don't worry, papa Ean is with you," I said trying to comfort him just as Stacy would comfort me on nights like this.

I pulled out the last scroll and read it out softly trying to quiet my mind. Exodus 13:11-16 read:

יא וְהָיָה כִּי-יְבִאֲךָ יְהוָה, אֶל-אֶרֶץ הַכְּנַעֲנִי, כַּאֲשֶׁר נִשְׁבַּע לְךָ, וְלַאֲבֹתֶיךָ; וּנְתָנָהּ, לָךְ.

יב וְהַעֲבַרְתָּ כָל-פֶּטֶר-רֶחֶם, לַיהוָה; וְכָל-פֶּטֶר שֶׁגֶר בְּהֵמָה, אֲשֶׁר יִהְיֶה לְךָ הַזְּכָרִים-- לַיהוָה.

יג וְכָל-פֶּטֶר חֲמֹר תִּפְדֶּה בְשֶׂה, וְאִם-לֹא תִפְדֶּה וַעֲרַפְתּוֹ; וְכֹל בְּכוֹר אָדָם בְּבָנֶיךָ, תִּפְדֶּה.

יד וְהָיָה כִּי-יִשְׁאָלְךָ בִנְךָ, מָחָר--לֵאמֹר מַה-זֹּאת: וְאָמַרְתָּ אֵלָיו--בְּחֹזֶק יָד הוֹצִיאָנוּ יְהוָה מִמִּצְרַיִם, מִבֵּית עֲבָדִים.

טו וַיְהִי, כִּי-הִקְשָׁה פַרְעֹה לְשַׁלְּחֵנוּ, וַיַּהֲרֹג יְהוָה כָּל-בְּכוֹר בְּאֶרֶץ מִצְרַיִם, מִבְּכֹר אָדָם וְעַד-בְּכוֹר בְּהֵמָה; עַל-כֵּן אֲנִי זֹבֵחַ לַיהוָה, כָּל-פֶּטֶר רֶחֶם הַזְּכָרִים, וְכָל-בְּכוֹר בָּנַי, אֶפְדֶּה.

טז וְהָיָה לְאוֹת עַל-יָדְכָה, וּלְטוֹטָפֹת בֵּין עֵינֶיךָ: כִּי בְּחֹזֶק יָד, הוֹצִיאָנוּ יְהוָה מִמִּצְרָיִם.
{ס}[§]

---

[§] "And it shall be when the LORD shall bring thee into the land of the Canaanite, as He swore unto thee and to thy fathers, and shall give it thee, that

After reading this commandment my mind felt like an ocean of clarity rushing in. I looked down at Tur who was nestled under the covers beside me looking up at me. I put the Tefillin and scrolls back in the bag and headed for the kitchen for olive oil and a glass of water. Tur was sitting up in bed when I returned to the room. I put the glass of water on the nightstand, opened the oil and placed my finger in the nozzle to moisten it. I reach over to Tur and anointed his head then mine. The fog rolled in.

"Thank you LORD."

I placed the oil down and grabbed the glass of water and the bottle of *Ambien* pills. Sitting on the edge of the bed I held the glass of water between my thighs as I opened the bottle of pills and

---

*thou shalt set apart unto the LORD all that openeth the womb; every firstling that is a male, ... And it shall be when thy son asketh thee in time to come, saying: What is this? that thou shalt say unto him: By strength of hand the LORD brought us out from Egypt, from the house of bondage; and it came to pass, when Pharaoh would hardly let us go that the LORD slew all the firstborn in the land of Egypt, both the first-born of man, and the first-born of beast; therefore I sacrifice to the LORD all that openeth the womb, being males; but all the first-born of my sons I redeem. And it shall be for a sign upon thy hand, and for frontlets between thine eyes; for by strength of hand the LORD brought us forth out of Egypt.'"*

poured a third of the bottle into my left palm. Tur sat still looking at me.

"Take these," I said as I inserted one pill into his mouth followed by the glass of water.

"What is this?" he asked as he spit the pills out as I inserted them.

"Eat these," I demand as he struggled with me and gagged.

I forced the pills into his mouth and made him swallow each and every one. The pills were literally rammed down his throat. When his portion of the pills was gone Tur quieted down and became somber. He laid out on the bed and I waited for him to die before I took my ration. Tur began to mumble as he dozed off. I reached down to listen to what he was saying. As I drew near Tur's words punctured my heart.

"Papa Stacy loves you," he whispered.

Pain welled up in my heart and tears streamed down my face. The fog lifted.

"Get up!"

I shook Tur as he drifted off. Sitting him up I took my finger and stuck it down his throat. Tur gagged and threw up cloudy water.

"Get up!"

Tur whined softly then drifted off. I picked up the phone and dial 911.

"What is your emergency?" asked the operator on the line.

"My son took a bottle of pills."

"Is he conscious?"

"No."

"Is he breathing?"

"His breathing is shallow."

"What is your name?"

I told her.

"Where are you located?"

I gave her my address and she asked me a few more questions as she dispatched an ambulance to the house.

"How old is he?"

"He's five."

"We'll be there shortly. Would you like to stay on the phone?"

"I have to check on him," I said as I put the phone down.

Lifting Tur of the bed I tried to walk him around but he was unresponsive. I carried him into the bathroom and turned on the cold water to the shower. I held him under the water but there is no response. His body was limp and unresponsive. The water ran off his body as I carried him through the house then stood in the living room holding him. There was a knock on the door. I carried Tur to the door and opened it. Brian walked in and took Tur out of my arms and carried him to the sofa. Two paramedics came in behind Brian and began to check Tur's vitals. The paramedics picked him up and ran out to the ambulance and drove off to the hospital. As the sirens blared and the flashing lights passed the window I noticed that it was still light out and sunny. Brian kneeled down beside me as I sat on the sofa.

"Are you alright?"

"I don't know. What is happening?" I asked as Brian got up off his knee and began to look around the house.

He walked into the bedroom and noticed the pill bottle sitting upright on the night stand with the glass of water. Brian looked at the *Tiffany* bag and picked it up to look in it then placed it back beside the bed on the floor. He heard the shower running and went into the bathroom stepping over the puddles of water and turned off the shower. He looked around and came back into the living room.

"Come with me."

"Where are we going?"

"To the hospital," said Brian as he grabbed my arm and lifted me off the couch and directed me into the back seat of the police car.

~ ~ ~ ~

Tur was wheeled into the emergency room at CVPH connected to an intravenous to help flush his system, a technique used when teenagers are brought to the emergency room for alcohol poisoning. In Tur's case, the drugs would have already dissolved and were making their way into his bloodstream. Dr. Braun was on call and immediately ordered gastric lavage to remove any unabsorbed *Ambien* from Tur's stomach. Tur was still unconscious when Dr. Braun looked him over and noticed that his blood pressure was extremely low. She also ordered activated charcoal to be pumped into his stomach and intestines to prevent the drug from being absorbed into his bloodstream, and a cathartic to help discharge it from his bowels. These procedures were all done without my consent, because it was a life and death situation. Dr. Braun had total control over Tur's life.

I, on the other hand, was ushered to the third floor for a psychological evaluation. I never liked psychologists. The offices of psychologists always had bizarre artwork. Every office I visited as a child hung paintings of faceless images in situations of peace. I used to believe it was a ploy on the therapist's part to get their patients to see themselves in those tranquil images to help quiet the mind. It was already too late. I had taken my flight of fancy, and during it I tried to murder my son. I was back now.

"They're just going to talk with you a bit," said Brian as he sat with me in the waiting room.

The door to the offices opened and out popped Dr. Ludwig. She was tall and pale with a short bob and steel rimmed glasses.

"I'll see you now," said Dr. Ludwig as she stepped back in behind the door. She was so tall her head almost hit the top of the door's metal frame.

I rose from the chair and followed the doctor to her office. The offices were very quiet. There didn't seem to be much going on compared to the emergency room. As we headed to her office I stopped before a painting. The image was geometric. Around the center of the painting were flowers made of rigid forms. The center of the painting consisted of a heart with a square and triangle on opposite ends. Dr. Ludwig noticed that I was not behind her. She stopped and turned around to wait for me. The figures in the painting came alive in three dimensions with the heart in the center turning black. It pumped and pulsed at me. The heart in my chest raced as Dr. Ludwig retraced her footsteps back to me. She stood beside me and looked at the painting. We stood still for a few moments until I asked.

"Why is the heart dark?"

Dr. Ludwig did not respond. She gently took my arm and guided me to her office. I was floating. Once again everything around me was clouded. The state seemed to be naturally induced. As we got closer to her office and farther away from the pulsing heart my vision and the space around me cleared. Psychologists are supposed to help their patients get to that place. Get to the clearing. As we walked through the hallway, I felt as if I was already there and I didn't even speak with the doctor yet. Dr. Ludwig led me into her office. The office décor was very mod. I took a seat across from its twin where the doctor sat.

"What brings you here?"

"My son took a bottle of pills this evening. No. I mean today," I said as the sun settled behind the doctor outside the window.

The sky was a burnt orange with purples and blues glowing from behind the clouds.

"Did it rain today?"

"Not at all, it has been quite a lovely day. Can you tell me a little bit about what happened?" asked Dr. Ludwig.

I thought for a while before I spoke.

"My son took some pills off my nightstand and ate them."

"Where were you?"

"I was watching television in the living room."

"When did you notice he ate some of the pills?"

"I did not realize he ate some of the pills until he walked out of the room wobbling and came to me and laid on my lap. It was out of the ordinary for him, so I went into the room and looked around and noticed the pills were opened on the bed."

"What did you do then?"

I told the doctor the true chain of events from the point when I began to tell Tur to get up and walked him around the room. The first part of the story obviously was all bull. The doctor began to give me a mental status and then went for the genealogy.

"Can you tell me more about your family?"

As I explained to the doctor my family tree she got up to get a pad and pen then sat back down. As she starts to draw symbols indicating my family tree and relations I lapsed into my relationship with Stacy and his recent passing.

"So you have had some recent stressful events?"

"You could say so."

After she compiled all the necessary information to make an initial diagnosis, she scheduled a follow-up visit, handed me an appointment card and escorted me back to the waiting area. As we exited into the waiting room she turned to Brian.

"May I speak with you?"

"Sure," said Brian as I took a seat and both of them disappeared behind the door.

When Brian reappears we both went to the emergency room to check on Tur. The head nurse on call informed us that he was transported to the ICU on the pediatric ward. We immediately went back upstairs to the ward and met up with Ms. Marcus, the social worker on his case.

"You cannot see him. You are not cleared."

Ms. Marcus was a large African American woman with a straight perm who approached in a bull dog stance.

"Can you at least tell me how he is doing?"

"I cannot give out medical information. I'll call the doctor," said Ms Marcus as she paged Dr. Braun.

I called Erica while we waited.

"It's me. Listen, Tur is in the hospital."

"What's wrong?"

"He took a bottle of pills."

"Is he alright?"

"They won't tell me anything yet. Can you come up?"

Erica was quiet for a moment.

"I'm sorry, but I can't."

"I need you here."

"Keep me posted on his condition. I have to go," said Erica and hung up the phone.

Dr. Braun approached me.

"This has been quite a few difficult years for you."

"How is he?"

"He's conscious."

"Can I see him?"

"I'll allow you to see him for a little while."

"Is he going to be alright?"

"We don't know. We need to keep him here for a while to make sure there is no neurological damage."

"Where is he?"

"Come."

Brian and I followed her to Tur's room. When I got to the room Tur was laying motionless in bed. I smiled at him but he did not respond. His body was still and his eyes followed me as I approached the bed. I stroked his head as Brian took a seat by the door.

"Ten minutes," said Dr. Braun as she turned around and disappeared down the corridor.

I stood beside Tur until the ten minutes were up. The whole time I was there he did not respond to me. He was pale and expressionless. Brian just sat watching me watch Tur. Dr. Braun came back into the room to let us know that time was up. I kissed Tur on the forehead as Brian got up from the chair. We left.

"I'll get you home," said Brian.

As we drove back to the house I remained silent. My head was starting to feel clouded again.

"You must be hungry."

"Yeah."

"Do you mind if we stop for a bite?"

"I can eat."

Brian pulled into the *Lone Diner*. When we got inside the hostess sat us in a booth by a window overlooking the parking lot. A waitress came over and took our order. Both Brian and I ordered breakfast and coffee.

"That was a pretty big scare you had today."

"Yeah."

"How are you holding in there?"

"It's hard with Stacy's passing."

"It gets easier. I lost my wife ten years ago next month."

"Sorry to hear. How did she go?"

"I lost her to lung cancer. She was a smoker. She went pretty quickly after the diagnosis."

"Was she in a lot of pain?"

"We both were, but I got through it and you will to."

"Do you have any other family?"

"I have a daughter who keeps me going. Although she is grown she is still my baby girl. I would have loved to have a son."

"Boys are tough," I said as the waitress served our food.

"Anything else I can get for you?" asked the waitress.

"We're good."

"You got to keep an eye on them."

"Uh?"

"Tur, you have to keep an eye on him."

"Yeah."

"How did he get into the pills?"

I stopped eating.

"The pills were on my nightstand. I was in the other room when he took them."

"What about the glass of water?"

My head became more clouded as Brian fired questions at me.

"Water?"

"There was a glass of water in the room sitting by the bottle of pills."

"I always leave a glass of water by the bed."

"Usually when kids get into things they're not supposed to, they make a mess."

"Yeah."

"The rest of the pills were neatly placed in the bottle on the night stand."

"I picked them up off the floor and put them all back in the bottle on the nightstand."

"Didn't you freak out when you realized he took the pills?"

"What are you getting at?"

"Tur is not your biological son, correct?"

"That's right."

"Are you familiar with the Cinderella Effect?"

"No."

"It's when adopted or stepchildren are mistreated or murdered by a non-biological parent."

"Are you suggesting I tried to hurt Tur?"

"Your story does not seem to match the scene."

My heart was beating and I began to breathe deeply. My gut response was to bolt but I tried to sit still. I reached over and picked up my glass of water to quench my dry mouth. Brian sat across from me eating his eggs as he studied my responses. I pulled out my box of *Altoids* and offer him one.

"No, thanks."

I popped one in my mouth and put the case back in my pocket.

"Would you mind taking me home now? I've been through enough."

"Sure. You know sometimes situations arise when man interferes with nature." said Brian as he reached into his pocket and pulled out his wallet to pay the bill.

He threw my words back at me. He remembered me from the morning Stacy and I stopped when *l'orignal* was caught in the brush on the side of the road. Brian got up from the booth and followed me out to the car. He drove me home that night as I remained silent. When I got home I went into the house and crawled into bed.

# Part III

# Partnering

# Chapter VIII

# The Bull

Ms. Marcus the hospital social worker contacted Child Protective Services (CPS) to investigate Tur's incident after she spoke with Brian. Ms. Barker, a CPS worker, arrived at the house two days later looking to speak with me. Again, I had to drag myself out of bed to answer the door. Her visit was unexpected. When I opened the door she introduced herself and flashed her agency identification card. I invited her in.

"I'm here to speak with you about the incident involving your child."

I motioned to her that she was welcome to take a seat at the kitchen table. She sat and for about twenty minutes fired questions at me regarding Tur's overdose.

"May I look around the house?"

"Is it necessary?"

"I'm required to take stock of your food supply for the child and see the living conditions."

I didn't want to appear non-cooperative.

"Sure."

Since we were already in the kitchen Ms. Barker started there. She got up from the kitchen table and headed for the refrigerator. She opened the door and scanned its contents then moved up to the freezer. Ms. Barker took a package of forms out of her bag and flipped though them to a specific sheet and made some notes. She moved on to the pantry and closets above the counter. Ms Barker stopped her investigation periodically to take notes as to what our food supply consisted of.

"May I see where the child sleeps?"

"He has his own room," I explained as I led her through the living room and into Tur's bedroom.

Ms. Barker did not say a word as she walked through the house inspecting every inch and taking notes.

"So what happens next?"

"I have to speak to the responding officer once again and file a final report," said Ms. Barker as I guided her to the door.

"Did I pass inspection?"

"Sorry, I can't comment just yet."

After Ms. Barker left I did not know what to do with myself. All I kept thinking about was what Brian had told her. Knowing that I looked as guilty as I currently felt, there was nothing that I could say or do that would rationalize and explain my behavior or would warrant forgiveness. I thought about calling Mark but did not want to push myself on someone who was no longer interested. He said he would be in touch. The one person I thought I could depend on abandoned me. I could not understand why Erica repelled from me one hundred and eighty degrees in the opposite direction. Everyone in my life was abandoning me at a time I need them the most. As I sat at the kitchen table I realized there was one person who did not truly leave me. I could hear Tur's words echo in my mind.

"Papa Stacy loves you."

I realized he could not run if I went to talk to him, so I got up from the table, got dressed and headed out to the cemetery.

It was a long drive. Rona had Stacy's body planted among the rest of her family. I drove the car into the cemetery and parked it on the side of the walkway near Stacy's plot. There were rows of large old oak trees separating the Jews from the Christians. The old cemetery was originally a Christian cemetery that was sectioned off into two large plots of land. Golden orange leaves separate both sections and made their way to the ground as the wind blew. It was early October and the leaves were just beginning to fall. Stacy's plot had a few leaves surrounding his gravestone. There were small rocks that had fallen off the stone that were left from his burial ceremony. I walked over and touched the monument so that I could feel him and let him know I was there. Reaching down I picked up three small rocks and piled them back on top of his monument. Stacy never told me what this act of tradition symbolized, however, he did instruct me never to bring flowers to a Jewish cemetery.

"You never bring more death to the dead." I remembered him saying.

The orange leaves contrasted beautifully with the plush green lawn and stone grey monuments. I began to pick them up from around his plot. The cemetery was not originally designed for Jews. The trees would not be here. The Jewish section was extended from the original Christian cemetery as the local Jewish community grew. I took a seat on the grass and leaned into the monument. The carvings and the date were so fresh. I stared at the leaves in my hand and followed the veins as they sprawled out to the pointed tips looking for patterns to explain life and my situation. There were no answers. I looked at Stacy's name on the stone and began to weep. I chocked back my words.

"I'm sorry."

Tears streamed down my cheeks. The leaves fell out of my hand as I released them to wipe my face.

"Please forgive me," literally fell on dead ears.

Obviously, there was no response. What more could I expect from the dead. I realized at that moment it was I who had to forgive myself for my own wrongdoing. It was my desire that willed Stacy and Tur into my life. It was I who wanted a child and it was I who tried to end his life, no one else. I had tampered with the course of nature and interfered with the natural flow of God's creation by trying to end life. As I come to the realization of my situation, the sky turned smoke grey and thunder clouds rolled in above me. My mind's weight lifted as the wind picked up and droplets of rain fell from the sky forcing me to get out of my head and the open cemetery. Lifting myself off the ground I gathered the leaves and grabbed one stone off the monument. I dashed to the car. The sky opened and the rain began to pour out of the sky as I drove back north to the hospital to see Tur.

When I arrived at the hospital the nurse at the front desk of the pediatric ward would not let me see him.

"We cannot allow you in to see him."

"Why can't I?"

"You will need to speak with Ms. Marcus the social worker first."

"Please let her know that I am here."

The nurse called Ms. Marcus to the front desk. Ms. Marcus came out of her office and approached the desk twenty minutes later.

"Please come to my office."

She had a serious look on her face and did not invite small talk.

"How is he?"

"I will call Dr. Braun to speak with you for a full medical report after we are done."

We entered her office and she walked directly behind her desk and took a seat.

"Please sit."

"Why can't I see him?"

"Tur told me yesterday that you gave him pills."

My heart began to pound and the beads of sweat formed on my forehead.

"What do you mean he said I gave him pills?"

"That's exactly what I said."

"What did he say?"

"Papa Ean gave me pills."

"He must be confusing it with the mints I sometimes give him."

"What mints?"

"Yes sometimes I give him an *Altoid*," I said as I reached into my pocket and pulled out my small metal box of mints.

"I'm sorry but we have to remove the child from your care until a full investigation is completed."

"This is ridiculous! I want to see my son."

"You can see him but I must supervise the visit. Is there anyone in your family who would be willing to care for the child as the investigation goes forward?"

"Yes, my sister."

"May I have her contact information?"

I gave Ms. Marcus Erica's address and number. She then escorted me to see Tur. When we walked into the room he smiled.

"Papa Ean!"

Tur tried to hop off the bed as I approached him.

"No, no stay in bed."

"Lay back," said Ms. Marcus.

He was out of the ICU and in a regular hospital room.

"He will be discharged to foster care for placement if you sister cannot take him for some reason."

"Why placement?" I shouted as Tur looked up at me nervous.

I have never yelled or shouted in front of him.

"There will have to be a hearing if you are charged."

"Charged with what!"

"EWOC."

"EWOC?"

"Endangering the welfare of a child, or worse, attempted murder."

"I know what the hell it means. This is ridiculous!"

"Please calm down or I'm going to have to ask you to leave."

"I'm calm!"

I turned to Tur.

"Papa Ean gives you mints right?"

"I think you should leave," said Ms. Marcus as she grabbed onto my arm.

"If I'm leaving I'm taking him with me," I said and pulled my arm out of her hand.

"You will only make matters worse. Please let the system run its course. You do want the child back?"

The tears came and I wept like a child.

"Come with me before we upset the child."

Ms. Marcus escorted me out of the room and back to her office.

"Papa Ean!" shouted Tur as we left the room and disappeared down the hallway.

Back in her office she went over the procedure with me and assures me that they would get to the truth of the matter.

"How long will this take?"

"I assure you it doesn't happen over night. We will contact your sister to transfer him to her care."

My cell phone rang.

"Excuse me," I said and answered my phone.

"Hello."

"It's me, Mark. Listen we are euthanizing the bull this evening."

"I'll be there shortly," I said and closed my phone.

Ms. Marcus' expression of sympathy fell off her face.

"I have to get going."

"We will let you know when he is in your sister's custody."

"Don't worry, I'll be there when it happens," I said and left the office.

On my way to the DEC I called Erica more desperate and in need than ever. She picked up the phone on the third ring.

"It's me. I know I've depended on you for quite some time but this time I really need you or I will lose Tur."

"I'm listening."

"I'm being investigated and CPS is taking Tur out of my custody. The social worker at the hospital will place him with strangers if you do not agree to take him. Can you please help me?"

"I don't understand. Why are you being investigated?"

"They think I had something to do with Tur taking the pills. You know how I give him mints sometime?"

"Yeah."

"Well, he told them that I gave him pills. They confused him."

"That sounds ridiculous."

"They are ready to discharge him back to Jeanine's agency for foster placement. Please!"

"I'll come up to get him."

"You can call Ms. Marcus. She is the social worker at the hospital. I gave her your information as well."

"I'll call her. Ean..."

"Yeah."

"I really need to talk to you about something."

"Is everything alright?"

"Yeah, but I can't talk now, Leo is walking through the door. I'll see you soon," said Erica and hung up the phone.

~ ~ ~ ~

I pulled into a visitor parking lot of the DEC looking for an empty parking spot. It was late afternoon and getting colder as the winter season drew near. The strong wind blew the bristles of the tall evergreens lining the front of the large DEC complex. I didn't really notice the building when I dropped Mark off during the summer month. When I entered the building I introduced myself to an officer at the front desk in the lobby and told him I was there to see Mark. He picked up a phone to let Mark know that I arrived. Five minutes later Mark came out to the lobby to greet me.

"Thanks for calling me."

"I told you I would let you know when the day came. Let's get to the lab. The doctor has already started the procedure," said Mark as I followed him to a large steel door.

Mark scanned his identification card across a small black box with a small red light that turned green and the door clicked as it unlocked. As I followed Mark to the DEC lab he explained how they were able to catch *l'orignal.*

"We found him back on I-87. We received a call that the moose was running back and forth along the road. He was quite aggressive when we approached and retrieved him. It took a lot to take him down. His aggressive behavior was typical of brain worm infection."

"Will I be allowed in?"

"You will have to suit up before I can bring you into the lab. We are in the process of extracting any semen we can so that we can study its motility and impregnate a few cows. This is the perfect time of year since we are in the beginning stages of the rut and the females will be in estrus soon. Come this way."

Mark brought me through a long corridor to another large battleship grey steel door and swiped us in. We made a left turn and continued down a long white hallway.

"We are approaching the lab," said Mark as he pointed to windows that allowed one to view the staff working on different concerns the DEC monitored.

There was a white sign with blue lettering that read Micro-Biology Laboratory.

"We will be there soon. This is our lab for testing E. Coli, Fecal Streptococcus, etc., you get the idea. The lab is 95% robotic. We test the water from New York City streams and rivers. We also test park swimming water," said Mark as he scanned his badge to open another door that led to the animal testing area.

The outer area of the lab was a small room comprised of lockers and benches for entrance preparation. Mark went over to a locker and took out equipment to suit up. He then went over to a large metal cabinet and pulled out a white meshed suit, rubber gloves, meshed slippers, and goggles for me. I put on the protective gear over my clothing then entered the lab where *l'orignal* was being held. *L'orignal* was lying on a large steel table with one of his hind legs held up by a hoist. He was surrounded by DEC research staff and the veterinarian performing the procedure. The veterinarian was extracting the last bit of semen from the moose then taped the incision that was made above the scrotum with surgical tape. The vet did not bother to suture him since the moose was going to be euthanized soon after.

My last night with Stacy he described to me the process he went through when he was making his deposit that helped produce Tur. He explained that after filling out a lengthy questionnaire he was led to a collection room with girly magazines and videos to get him started. After an initial sample was collected to test how much sperm was in his emission and how it froze, he was invited back to provide an additional sample, blood work and a full physical. It was not a one shot deal. Stacy was required to give a sample a few times a month for six months. All of this just to become a full fledged fraternity member.

After the semen was extracted the vet began the euthanizing process by first inserting a needle that pumped more sedative into *l'orignal*, and then the euthanizing solution. The process took about an hour. Once *l'orignal* was gone the vet called the time and the staff cleared the room. Mark and I approached the moose as it laid there still. Mark lowered the hoist that held its hind leg.

"Are you sure you don't want the remains to sell off?"

"No thank you. We didn't kill it, they did."

I walked up to the edge of the table where the moose's head laid and touched its antlers that had grown back since the last time I had seen it. I stroke the moose's cheek.

"Is it alright to take off my glove? I wanted to feel its coat."

"That's alright. The brain worm cannot be transferred to humans."

I peeled off the plastic glove and ran my hand over the moose's coat. Saliva began to drip out of the moose's mouth. Mark and I just stared at the moose for a while. In my mind, I kept on saying I forgive you as I stroked the moose's fur.

Mark then broke the silence.

"Would you like to grab a bite to eat? I was so excited about having the moose here that I didn't eat lunch."

"Sure, I could use some company."

"Let's get going. The staff has to get the moose transported for cremation."

"That's what Stacy wanted."

"Was it done?"

"I defied his wishes and had him buried instead."

"Let's go," said Mark as I followed him out of the lab."

~ ~ ~ ~

Erica hung up the phone then walked over to the south wall of her studio that supported the pile of empty ecru canvasses and selected one. She could hear Leo climbing the stairs to the studio as she walked over to the easel and mounted the canvas, locking it in place with the top support. Erica was following her muse. She was moved to work in oils. Erica whipped off her paint blotter encrusted in a dry coat of acrylics. She grabbed a few tubes of acrylic colors when Leo walked in. Leo smiled at Erica as he entered the room. His mood had improved since Erica returned Tur to me. Leo always found pleasure in seeing Erica engulfed in the act of creation. He was proud that he could afford her the luxury to engage in what she loved to do most. What he did not know, however, was that Erica had developed a new found passion that only motherhood could bring.

Leo approached her from behind as she stood in front of the easel clutching the acrylics. He wrapped his arms around her. Leo whispered in her ear.

"How's my wife tonight?"

"She's fine."

"How was your day?"

"Not too busy. It's always slow this time of year."

"I think the cold slows things down."

This explained why he was home a half hour earlier than usual. Erica was not expecting him home so soon. Nor was she expecting to tell him that Tur would be staying with them once again.

"What would you like for dinner tonight?" asked Leo as he squeezed into Erica.

Erica allowed him to hold her longer than she wished hoping he will be comforted for the blow of information she is about to deliver to him.

"I love to see you paint."

Erica pulled away and grabbed on to him with her free hand. She guided him to the table to take a seat and put down the paints.

"Honey, I need to talk with you."

"What is it?"

Erica had prepared for this moment. She took a deep breath and let it out. Before she spoke her face blushed.

"I wanted you to know…"

"What is it?"

Leo's face grew concerned. Erica looked into his eyes and told him.

"My brother called today and asked if we could mind Tur for a while."

"How long will it be this time?"

"They might be taking Tur away from him. He really needs us this time."

"I'm OK with it."

Erica was surprised. She did not expect Leo to react in the way that he did.

"You seem to be in good spirits."

"I always am when I see my wife in the act of creation."

Erica thought to herself how she may have looked a few nights ago when she and Leo were making up after she had brought Tur back home to me. When Leo had mentioned the words separation and divorce, Erica stopped taking her monthly precautions without telling him.

"Are you ready for dinner?"

"Let me take you out, your choice. Your wish is my command."

Erica paused for a moment.

"Let's have Mediterranean."

"Sounds good," said Leo as he rose from his stool, grabbed Erica's hand and guided her out of the studio.

As Erica was being led away from the studio she looked back at the lost moment and opportunity to tell Leo what she truly had intended to, that she is three weeks pregnant.

~ ~ ~ ~

Mark sat across from me sipping a glass of water. The waiter took our order and filled our glasses. The restaurant overlooked Saranac Lake. A fire was burning in the center of the room. This area of New York had the coldest temperatures this time of the year. It was late October, Halloween day to be exact. As I sat with Mark I wondered if they would be having a party at the hospital on the pediatric ward. As far as I knew, Tur was still there.

"What are you thinking about?"

"Just wondering if they will be having a party at the hospital on the ward where my son is."

"They usually hold parties for kids during the holidays," Mark reassured me so that I would relax.

The jack-o-lantern, black cat and witch cut outs on the walls of the restaurant shifted my attention.

"You never told me how you and Stacy met."

I picked up an orange and green gourd off the table and rolled it in my hand.

"No big story. I was out drinking one night trying to forget about things when he approached me and asked me if I wanted to dance. I was already a bit plastered and almost fell off the bar stool following him to the dance floor. We danced for a few beats and then the music changed to a slow dance. I opted out and we sat together and talked all night."

"I try not to get involved with guys I meet at a bar. It usually doesn't work out."

"Well, it worked out for me until the accident."

"How many years were you two together?"

"Fourteen."

"I think we lasted so long because I was Stacy's rescue case."

"What do you mean?"

"When I met Stacy I was a bit of a drinker."

"You mean an alcoholic?"

"Yeah, you could say that."

"Stacy never drank and I learned from him that I didn't need to, especially when things get tough."

"I had a few relapses but then one day I just woke up and didn't need it any more. The night he died I promised him I would not drink."

"Why so rigid?"

"I could not keep the promise."

"Life is not like that."

"My family members are heavy drinkers. I ran away from the madness. My sister Erica turned to art. It allows her to have control over something in her life while losing herself. I allow others to gain control over me. It's my symptom of a child of an alcoholic. That is why Stacy and I were such a perfect fit."

"You were his Geisha moose."

"I guess."

"While you are with me I will ensure that you are pure bull," said Mark as the waiter served him a large plate of baked ziti and me a steaming plate of eggplant Parmesan with a side of spaghetti.

"Can we have an order of garlic bread?"

The waiter nodded and left the table. As we ate Mark asked me more questions about my past and how I would describe myself as a person. When I tried to ask him questions he reflected them like a female cow rejecting the advances of a male bull. The waiter brought over our bread. He was not letting me have the opportunity to get close or know about his life. I was being led to run around in my mind and share my sporadic thoughts as bulls run during the rut. He was not letting me get an inch into who he was. He was not ready.

"I found you attractive the moment I saw you at the pharmacy."

"Thank you for sharing that and being so straight forward."

When we were done eating our entre we share a cannoli. The fact that he was sharing it with me gave me a glimmer of hope that he would select me as a mate. When the waiter came over with the bill, Mark pulled out plastic and insisted on paying. I thanked him then took the opportunity to ensure another date.

"Can I make you dinner some time next week?"

He reflected the invitation.

"I'll call you and let you know when I am available."

"Good," I said as we left the restaurant.

Because Mark and I had taken separate cars to the restaurant we said our goodbyes in the parking lot and went our separate ways. When I got home there was a message on the answering machine. I pressed the button.

"Mr. Ean. It's me Saudi. Please call me when you get this message. I have some information for you about Claudia."

The next day I got up out of bed and readied myself for the day. I was in better spirits since my night out with Mark. There was nothing really for me to do. I thought about contacting the hospital to find out if Ms. Marcus was able to reach Erica, but I knew Erica would have called me the moment she heard from the hospital. As I walked through the house I found myself drawn to Tur's room. I entered the room. The bed was still in the same condition it was when he was transported to the hospital. His blanket was still in my room. I straightened the sheet on the bed then moved over to the desk. The journal Stacy had left behind was in the drawer. I took it out and sat down. Everything around me felt soft. I ran my fingers along the spine of the fabric journal and looked at the embryo on the cover before I opened it. The pen was still in the book where I had left it. It was the same pen that I took out of Stacy's hand the morning I woke up beside his stiff body. I started to write the events that have occurred since the funeral. The writing came out in spurts. I took a few breaks to make a pot of coffee and get refills. The writing stopped a little after noon when the phone rang. The phone rang a fourth time before I could get to it.

"Hello Mr. Ean."

"Hi Saudie, what's going on?"

"You asked me to call you if anything new happens with Claudia's case."

"There's new activity?"

"A judge won't give Tur to her."

"Why do you say that?"

"You know by the file that I faxed you she never finished the treatment program."

"I haven't had a chance to read the file."

"Don't bother because there was a new arrest."

"Did you say a new arrest?

"Yes."

"What for?"

"The same bag of tricks. She is charged with a felony criminal possession of illegal substances and weapons charge."

"When did this happen?"

"Three days ago. It's an open and shut case for the ADA. She is a predicate and no judge will release her on bail. She is once again facing a felony criminal possession of illegal substances, weapons charge and resisting arrest. The officers wrote in their statement that she was transporting a large quantity of crack and crystal methamphetamine."

"In Stacy's words she's fucked."

"Do you need me to fax the paper to you?"

"Please!"

"I have to get back to work."

"You're wonderful!" I said to Saudi then hung up the phone.

I was juiced. My date with Mark was hopeful and now the information on Claudia was making me high. I called Lavonda with the good news but she did not answer so I hung up. Thinking about what Mark said to me during our first date made me realize that Tur was the situation that I wanted.

There were only two obstacles left, Rona and Brian. I grabbed my coat and left. My goal was to tackle Brian first, so I drove to the New York State Troopers Office off Interstate-87.

There was only one vehicle in the parking lot when I arrived. I parked beside it and went inside the brown log cabin style building. The station was dark. There was a beam of light coming from the office in the far left corner of the station. I walked toward the office and could see a Trooper sitting with his hat tilted down and his feet on a chair beside the desk he was sitting behind. It was Brian. He was taking an afternoon lunch nap. When I walked up to the door I noticed a half eaten Turkey club on his desk resting on *Saran Wrap* and a *Sierra Mist*. He was snoring softly. I knocked on the door frame. Brian lifted his head and pulled his feet off the chair. He seemed extra surprised that it was me.

"Can I talk to you?"

"Sure, come in."

I approached the desk and took the seat beside it. My hand brushed the top of the seat before I sat down.

"How can I help you?" said Brian as he took of his hat and placed it on the desk beside the sandwich.

The one florescent light that was on above his desk illuminated his dark silky black hair. His blue eyes twinkled at me as I inhaled. He was much older than I. Brian aged very well and his youthful looks were well preserved. I didn't remember him looking this good the night we discussed Tur's incident at the diner. His looks were drawing me in. I sat up in my chair and

focused my attention on him. Even though he was
the impetus for the whole investigation against me,
at that moment I found myself drawn to him.

"I wanted to talk with you about what you
were implying at the diner the other night."

"Go on."

"I just wanted to let you know that I would not
intentionally hurt my son."

"I see."

"The social worker at the hospital told me that
there would be a full investigation."

"There is."

"My custody of Tur is being challenged and I
do not want to lose him."

A feeling of empowerment engulfed me as I
spoke those words, but apart of me was having a
difficult time still believing them.

"Go on."

Brian's two word responses were intense and
gave me the impression that he was stonewalling
me. My gut reaction was to appease him.

"Please don't take this wrong, but you have
very nice eyes. They are so crystal blue."

Finally, I expressed what I wanted him to
know back at the hospital before Dr. Braun
interrupted us. Brian blushed and grabbed his hat
and placed it back on his head tugging on the
front tip of it to shade his eyes.

"My report has already been submitted," said
Brian as I sank back into the chair.

"I really don't want to lose my son."

Brian's chair sat on four wheels. He rolled
himself from behind the desk and over to the chair
I was sitting on and sat directly in front of me.
Brian leaned forward into my space and placed his

hand on mine that was resting on my lap. My heart began to beat harder. I could feel the pumping on my chest wall. I nervously smiled.

"Initially, I thought you were giving me some bull story. I can hear you honestly don't want to lose your son."

I sat up and pulled my hand from his. His hand landed on my thigh and he slowly pulled it off towards him.

"I have to get going," I said and got up from the chair.

Brian also rose and stood directly in front of me. I stared into his chest and could see it rise and fall. Our bodies were an inch apart when I turned away towards the door.

"I'll show you out."

Brian placed his hand on my shoulder and released it. He walked me to the door and stepped ahead of me to open it.

"Please, let me know if you need anything."

"I will," I said and I left the station and quickly walked to my car trying to make sense of what just happened.

Brian watched me and tipped his hat as I got into my car and drove off crossing Interstate-87 heading south to Erica's.

# Chapter IX

## Copulation

When I arrived at Erica's she was working on the painting she was about to begin the other day when Leo got home. Her front door was open so I let myself in. Knowing she would be in her studio I went straight up the stairs. When I walked into her studio Erica was standing before her easel. Erica held a small thin paint brush in one hand and a mosaic encrusted paint blotter in the other. She was making long fine strokes of blue and green. An image of the ocean and the sky meeting appeared as one at the top of the canvass. Her painting looked hopeful until she pressed the tip of the brush in a glob of dark brown paint and stroke the canvas streaking the paint along what looked like a serene ocean. The image turned as violent as her forceful strokes. She was so entranced into the painting Erica did not see me enter the room.

"Hey."

My voice startled her. She turned to me with eyes wide open. The intensity of her gaze was focused in my direction.

"What are you doing here?"

"I just thought I would stop by."

"I received a call from the social worker. They're scheduled to drop off Tur early this evening."

"I'm really glad you and Leo can help out."

"Really, don't think you're allowed to be here. You have to make an appointment with the agency first if you want to see him."

Erica walked over to her work table. She set the brush on top of the blotter and placed them both down. Erica wiped her hands on her shirt. I walked over to the table and sat down. There was a small tea set on the table. Erica poured me a cup of tea.

"How are things with Leo?"

"Things seem to be getting better, but we will see how things go when Tur gets here."

"He is still jealous of Tur?"

"I think so."

"You said you had something to tell me."

Erica poured a cup of tea for herself. The steam rose from the cup as she lifted it to her mouth and gently blew over the rim. She sipped the hot liquid and placed the cup back on the table taking in a deep breath.

"Leo mentioned separating a few weeks ago."

That explained her behavior and why she quickly dropped Tur off.

"You guys are not going to divorce."

"He just mentioned it."

"Don't worry. You guys will work things out."

My narcissism and self-centeredness did not allow her the opportunity to share with me her true struggle until I shared with her my own demons.

"I hope so..."

Erica was about to continue when I cut her off.

"You know my situation with Tur."

"What about it?"

"I was the one responsible."

"It's not your fault the baby took the pills off your nightstand."

"No, I was responsible."

"What are you saying?"

"I gave Tur the pills."

Erica stopped drinking her tea and looked at me.

"How could you?"

"It just happened. I didn't know what I was doing."

"That is what all this is about? I thought it was an accident."

"So does everyone except me. They have me seeing a psychiatrist."

"What did they say?"

"My second visit is tomorrow. I think there is something wrong with me."

"You think?"

"I went to talk with the Trooper who took the report of the incident. He mentioned the Cinderella Effect."

"I never heard of it."

"It has something to do with non-biological parents harming their children. Don't know if they are going to charge me with a crime. He mentioned an endangerment charge or attempted murder."

"How could you do such a thing?"

"I told you, I don't know. My mind was clouded. I've really been depressed since Stacy's been gone."

"They should be here soon. You're going to have to leave before Tur gets here."

"I'll go."

"How is anyone supposed to trust you?"

"You can trust me."

I grabbed Erica's arm.

"How can I know," said Erica as her face strained.

Erica could not hold it in any longer.

"How can I trust you with my child?"

"Tur is not your child."

"Ean, I'm pregnant."

"What?"

"I'm going to have a baby."

"How can I trust you with my child, let alone Tur?"

Erica's words hit me hard. I never thought she would ever talk to me that way. She was changing.

"Does Leo know?"

"I haven't told him yet."

"Didn't you both agree that you were not going to have children?"

"You know it was part of our agreement before we got married."

"When are you going to tell him?'

"Soon. Abortion is not an option. I want to see how he reacts to Tur being with us."

"Did you once tell me never use a child like a pawn? It only hurts the child."

Erica looked at me and realized I was right. Those were her words not mine.

"I'll tell him tonight."

The tea went right through me. I got up to use the bathroom. When I returned Erica was pouring herself another cup. The edges of her mouth formed a deep frown. I had to change the subject. I stood at the edge of the table.

"Rona called."

"What did she want?"

"I don't know. I didn't call her back."

"You can't deny the child his grandmother."

"I'm hoping she doesn't show up for the hearing."

"We'll see."

"Call me when Tur gets in. I'm going to head back up north," I said, "You know when it is?"

"When the hearing is?"

I nodded and reached over the table to hug her.

"I'll see you later. I love you."

"Congratulations. I love you," I said as I left her there sipping her tea.

~ ~ ~ ~

Dr. Ludwig was escorting a patient out of her office when I arrived. Before entering her office I stopped by the pediatric ward to see if Tur was still there. The nurse at the desk informed me he was discharged the previous evening. It must have been late because Erica never phoned to tell me as I had requested. Dr Ludwig saw me entering the waiting room.

"I'll see you now."

I followed her into her office. Everything around me looked vaguely familiar. The only thing I was sure to recognize were the faceless paintings that hung on the walls and particularly the one with the black heart. When I passed the dark heart there was a pulse, a single heart beat was heard. It was the life force. I remembered Stacy's creation story. He said creation was from the heart and of God. This time when I saw the heart, it was the color indigo with red shadings. The heart was no longer black. I saw myself in that painting. Unlike the guardians with no faces I was able to project my subconscious mind onto the image. Catching up to Dr. Ludwig I entered the room and took the same seat as my first visit.

"So how are you doing?"

My words gushed. After telling her the story of Tur and where I was in that situation I went on to tell her about meeting Mark and what I wanted out of my relationship with him. When I digressed to Erica's problems with Leo, Dr. Ludwig refocused me back to my life. Before my time was about up I was feeling comfortable enough to talk about Stacy and what it felt like to lose him.

"I miss him."

"Who's him?"

"Stacy."

"We can talk about him during our next session," said Dr. Ludwig and scribbled a new date on an appointment card and handed it to me, "See you then."

I thanked the doctor and left her office. As I walked to the car my cell phone rang. It was Mark.

"I'm free for dinner tomorrow night."

The cell phone fell from my ear as I tried to catch it while Dr. Ludwig's card was in the same hand. I caught the phone and placed it back to my ear.

"Sorry about that. Is there anything specific you would like me to make?"

"Surprise me. I'll see you at eight," said Mark and hung up.

~ ~ ~ ~

Erica waited for Leo to come home. She just finished feeding Tur a can of ravioli and a glass of milk for dinner and sat him down in front of the television to watch an after school special. It was getting late. Leo recently told her that things were slowing down at the office and he was starting to get home early until he found out Tur would be staying with them. Tur got up from the floor in the living room and approached Erica who was sitting on the sofa.

"When will I see Papa Ean?"

"Honey, we will see him soon."

"When?"

"We have to go to court next week. We will see him then."

"That's far away?"

"I promise you we will see him soon," said Erica as Leo walked through the front door.

Leo came into the living room. Tur turned and saw Leo approaching Erica and went back to his spot on the floor. Erica rose from the sofa. Leo approached Erica and kissed her on the cheek.

"Work picking up again?"

"No, it's still quiet."

"Why so late today?"

"I went to the station to vacuum out the car."

"Are you hungry? I pulled out some ground beef for burgers."

"That sounds good."

Erica grabbed onto Leo's hand and led him to their country style kitchen. Leo took a seat at the oak table while Erica walked over to the sink to wash her hands. She dried them off with a towel hanging over the sink and went over to the counter to prepare the burgers. In a mixing bowl she dumped ground beef, some spices and chunks of garlic then molded the meat into two large patties. After making the patties she rinsed her hands once again, placed a skillet on the gas stove and turned on the burner to the high setting. The patties sizzled as she placed them on the hot skillet. When the burgers were medium rare she served Leo. As they sat and eat Tur entered the room.

"Can I have more milk?"

Leo looked at him as he bites into his burger showing his incisors. Tur flashed a look at him and turned away focusing on Erica.

"I'll make you some hot chocolate when we're done, OK?"

"Yes."

"You can go inside now," instructed Leo.

Erica looked at Leo with disappointment.

"Has your brother let you know when he is going to come and get him?"

"The court hearing is next week."

"Why do you treat him the way you do? He likes you."

"You know I'm not good with kids."

"Will you send our child into the next room when you don't what it around?"

"We don't have kids."

"He is not a goat, he is a child."

Leo took his final bite of his burger when Erica could no longer keep her secret in.

"I'm pregnant."

"You're what?"

"I'm going to have our child."

"I thought you said we were never going to…"

"It's done. We created it together."

"How long have you known?"

"I just found out earlier this week. Does it really matter?"

Leo still had a few remnants of beef in his cheeks and swallowed. He got up from his chair and went over to Erica. She held a face full of fear and tears welled up in her eyes. Leo pulled his arm back out wide and the force of his arm went forward. Erica cringed as Leo's arm wrapped around her. He pulled her near and hugged her with great force as they both cried.

"I love you so much," said Leo as the tears streamed down both of their faces.

Erica choked back her words and released them in one big blow.

"I love you to."

What Erica did not know was that Leo wanted a child of his own but did not tell her. When they met it was Erica who first expressed that she did not want to have children out of fear that they would grow up to be alcoholics like the rest of her family members. Leo loved her so much that he sacrificed his true desires so that she would have the life that she thought she wanted. He knew her art was just a substitute. Most of her paintings were made using soft pink, blue, yellow and green pastels. He couldn't bring himself to tell her his analysis because he did not want to shatter her living reality.

"Let's take Tur out for some chocolate ice cream," said Leo as he lifted her out of her chair and kissed her passionately.

"It's too cold out for ice cream."

"It never too cold for ice cream," said Leo, "And never say never."

~ ~ ~ ~

I picked up some groceries to make a vegetarian chili for Mark on my way home from Erica's. Mark sat across from me in the kitchen as I stirred the pot of chili. After I served the chili and we ate, Mark was full of compliments.

"This is delicious."

"I'm glad you liked the surprise."

Mark smiled at me.

"We found a surrogate female for the bull's sperm."

"Oh."

After eating, I got up and cleared the table.

"I'll help you with those."

"No that's alright," I said as I placed the dishes in the sink to soak.

Mark's eyes followed me around the kitchen as I put the leftovers in the refrigerator. When I was done I walked over to Mark and took his hand and led him into the living room. We sat together on the sofa a section apart. His face was glowing.

"We are going to inseminate tomorrow. The cow is in estrus, I thought you would want to know."

Mark was always radiant when the topic of discussion was moose.

"You're certainly a moose man."

"They're my life."

"What else do you do besides skydiving and drinking?"

"I'm pretty much a home body. I grew up not too far from these parts. There is not much to do up north but enjoy nature."

"Have you ever been to the big city?"

"No, I really never traveled south of Plattsburgh."

"You're real country folk."

"I was raised on a farm about an hour west of here north of a little place called Churubusco. It's off state route 189 on the Canadian border. My family raised dairy cows and horses. Raising farm animals is what helped me find out and develop to who I am. I would get excited when assisting my father help the horse's mate. I would have to direct the male sex organ to help the process of copulation."

"Scarred for life?"

"It was a yearly event I looked forward to. You can say I bonded well with the male species ever since. My family depended on it to help increase the live stock on the farm to sell off. We only kept a pair of horses until we could no longer breed them, then we traded up for a younger pair. Horses are not like cattle. They don't produce anything that can be sold. You only make a profit if you sell them outright."

Marks face was still glowing. It seemed talking of any livestock excited him. He took a close look at my face and focused in on my eyes.

"You have eyes shaped like a doe's."

Heat rushed to my head. I turned away as Mark touched the side of my face and leaned in to kiss me. As he drew near I faced him and closed my eyes. His lips softly pressed against mine. I wanted to kiss him back. I thought it was too soon. Slowly I pulled back and turned away.

"Is everything alright?"

"Yes."

Mark inched closer to me and put his arm around my shoulders.

"I like being in your company."

He leaned into my neck and gently sucked on it. His suction was soft, not like the vampire's I met the night I was out at the Raw Hide avoiding Stacy.

"Don't know if I'm ready for this."

"I'm ready for you," said Mark as his left hand reached up to my chin and guided my face to his lips.

As he kissed me I returned his advances with greater force. Our heads bobbled side to side as his tongue lashed out onto mine. My body trembled. Mark stopped kissing me for a brief moment and got up from the sofa. He pulled me up to him and into the bedroom. I hesitated and become ambivalent when I saw the hospital bed in the room. As we stood before the bed Mark began to kiss me more passionately and ran his hands over my body. When his fingers reached the bottom of my shirt he grabbed it and yanked it off my body and over my head. He tossed the shirt to the floor as his arms resumed their position on my body with magnetic force. My arms held him tight as he pulled me closer to the bed. Mark undressed me. As he stood beside the bed undressing down to his boxers I slide onto the bed and underneath the covers. Mark pulled the weight of his body over mine and began to lap my body. Out of the corner of my eye I could see the sun fully setting as Mark made his way to the rise south of my border. From what Mark was showing me I decipher he was not your typical bull. Our love making lasted longer than the average time I had become accustomed to with Stacy. We stayed up until the next morning laughing and exploring each other's bodies. I told Mark about Tur's "accident" and that I had to attend the hearing. He offered to go with me. By that time we both stopped talking and tired out, it was three o'clock in the morning.

The alarm clock read eleven the next morning when I opened my eyes. The sun was up and rays of sunshine filled the room. As I climbed out of the bed Mark opened his eyes.

"What time is it?"

"It's a minute after eleven."

"Eleven," repeated Mark as he jumped out of the bed and searched around the bed for his clothes.

"Slow down!"

"Don't want to miss the insemination."

"We took care of that last night."

"Don't be nasty. You want to come."

I looked at Mark as he struggled with his sox.

"Took care of that also," I said with a grin on my face.

"Stop joking around."

"Sure."

"C'mon get dressed."

I too started to pick up my clothes and dressed. Mark followed me into the bathroom to wash up. He squeezed an inch of toothpaste on his index finger and brushed his teeth. We rinsed out our mouths, splashed water on our faces, and checked our hair. After we were done I grabbed my keys off the kitchen counter. Mark pushed me out the front door. I started to laugh out loud as he nudged me on. My laughter stopped when I saw Brian climb out of his trooper vehicle and shut the door. We climbed down the porch steps as Brian approached. As he witnessed us joking around Brian looked annoyed.

"Hey Brian," shouted Mark.

Brian did not respond. He looked at us like a disappointed parent and turned to me.

"Need to speak with you."

I turned to Mark.

"I'll meet you there. Stall them for me."

"Come soon. I hope we're not too late."

Mark got into his car and drove off.

"What was he doing here?" asked Brian.

"He came to see me about the moose that killed Stacy."

"You seemed to be joking around about something."

"Nothing at all," I said clearly lying to his face.

Brian took a deep breath and looked at me in disappointment then stared at the ground.

"What did you want to speak to me about?"

"You do want your son back?" asked Brian as he turned away and stormed off to his car.

"What is it?

Brian ignored me and got back into his car, turned on the ignition and drove off.

"Aw fuck!"

I got into my car and drove to the DEC hoping to make the insemination. As I drove Brian's behavior played over in my mind. I thought about him holding my hand while I was back in his office. Was this his way of consoling the people he came into contact with who experience a loss and was in crisis? Then it dawned on me that he was interested in me. It made sense that he would react that way with me after he came down hard on me at the diner. Unless, I thought, he was still trying to manipulate me to get at the truth.

~ ~ ~ ~

Mark came to pick me up the morning of the hearing. When he drove up I opened the driver's seat.

"I want to drive."

"Do you know how to drive a stick?"

Looking at Mark, I smiled.

"Didn't you learn that about me the other night you were over?"

Mark returned the smile and climbed out of the car.

"This is your first time in a big city. I don't want you to get lost."

"Fine with me," said Mark as he climbed into the passenger's side of his car.

My fear of driving had dissipated. Three hours later I drove into Albany on Route 787. Mark was amazed by the Albany skyline.

"This is nothing wait until we get to New York City."

I took the Clinton Avenue exit and drove up to the Family Courthouse and parked in front. Mark and I were late. Erica, Tur, Lavonda, Jeanine, Ms. Marcus, Ms. Barker and to my surprise Brian were already in the courtroom. Mark and I walked up to Erica and Tur who was surprised to see me. Ms. Barker informed Erica that she would have to mind Tur while the proceeding was in progress.

"Papa Ean!"

I was allowed to hug Tur. He was then passed off to Ms. Barker who walked over to the other end of the bench. Judge Lamb and his clerk were already on the bench waiting for all parties. I said hello to everyone and introduced them except Brian to Mark. Brian sat in the second row of benches holding his hat looking wounded. He glanced at Mark then at me as we took a seat.

"Are all parties present?" asked Judge Lamb.

Lavonda approached the bench.

"Your Honor, we are awaiting the petitioner."

"Are there not two?"

"Judge, the petition from the biological mother has been withdrawn. She is currently serving a long sentence at Bedford Hills. The open petition was filed by the biological grandmother."

"Are they here?"

"No."

"Let's give them a few more minutes," said the Judge as he got up and walked off the bench into his chambers.

Lavonda sat back down at one of two small tables in front of the courtroom.

Rona and Aton walked in the courtroom five minutes later. Aton looked as if he was being dragged into the room against his wishes. He was nicely dressed in a grey pin stripped Hugo Boss suit. Aton loves criminal law but he could not muster up the enthusiasm for the family court if his life depended on it. Although finely dressed, he looked like a cat that was just pulled out of a tub of water. Rona was wearing a tailored black Donna Karan pencil lined skirt. They both approached the clerk.

"We're a little late, we apologize."

The clerk rose and went into chambers to retrieve the judge. Lavonda got up from her seat and walked over to Aton to introduce herself. They both shook hands. Lavonda returned to her seat as Aton and Rona sat at the other small table. The Judge returned to the bench and began the proceeding. Aton approached and introduced himself to the court as counsel and the biological grandparent of the child in question. Rona got up and grabbed on Aton's jacket arm to speak to him. Aton pulled away.

"Shhh!"

"Please proceed," instructed Judge Lamb.

Aton began an opening statement that only the rich could afford in an attorney. He went on to describe what life was like raising his son Stacy then shifted to what it was like to lose his only son to a gay lifestyle and then a second time to the accident. Aton then went on to describe how he came to learn that Tur was their biological grandchild. He turned to face me and thanked me before the court. Then he really turned. Aton went into a discussion on the morality of homosexuality and the lifestyle his son had chosen.

"That is not the lifestyle he was designed by the creator to live."

Mark lets out a grunt. I quickly grab his hand and whisper to him."

"Respect the court."

Brian watched our interaction from the back row. By now he knew we were a couple.

"I will not have my grandchild be raised in such an environment."

Judge Lamb interrupted.

"Excuse me counsel but that will be for this court to decide! If there is nothing further I would like to hear from the respondent's counsel."

Lavonda cleared her throat, rose from her seat and approached the bench.

"Thank you, Judge Lamb."

She began with a description of how Stacy and I met. How we had come to love one another and our decision to adopt Tur. Lavonda was honest in that I did not learn of Tur's existence and that he was Stacy's biological child until after the foster care arrangement. She went on to explain that I went through with the foster care arrangement not knowing that Tur was Stacy's biological child and cared for the child when the biological mother had given him up for adoption. Lavonda stressed that I loved Tur even before I learned the child was my spouse's biological child. Rona shouted out.

"We would have also taken him in if we had known sooner!"

Judge Lamb lifted and slammed down his gavel.

"Ma'am, you're out of order!"

Aton turned to Rona and raised his hand.

"Shhh!"

Everyone in the courtroom looked. Lavonda finished her argument.

"I understand there was a recent incident that almost cost the child his life?" asked Judge Lamb.

Lavonda turned to Jeanine and Ms. Barker. Ms. Barker motioned to Jeanine to mind Tur as she approached the bench. My heart began to race.

"You're Honor, we have conducted a full investigation of the custodial parent and the child's living conditions. I must report today that they were actually quite remarkable in comparison to what we normally see. We have also conducted various interviews including one with State Trooper Flannery who is in the courtroom today. Mr. Flannery was the responding officer to the incident on the day of its occurrence and we have come to the conclusion that the report is unfounded."

My heart stopped beating for a second them resumed. My throat turned to stone as a tear streamed down my face. I turned around to Brian as I wiped my face and whispered.

"Thank you."

Brian face softened as he nodded his head.

"Your honor we have had no knowledge of an investigation," said Aton.

"Counsel at this point in time it is a moot issue," said Judge Lamb, "If there is nothing else I would like to speak to the child myself in chambers."

Judge Lamb got up from the bench followed by the clerk and both went through the side door behind the bench. Ms. Barker took Tur by the hand and led him behind the Judge followed by Ms. Marcus. The court officer exited chambers and waited with both parties in the courtroom until the judge returned. Forty minutes later Judge Lamb returned to the bench followed by everyone else that was in the room. The judge addressed the court but first invited both parties to make any comments; however, he made it clear that the court had reached its decision. Both Aton and Lavonda declined.

"Well then," said Judge Lamb, "Out of all my past custody cases this one is unique in that it will set a precedent in the State of New York for future custody disputes regardless of what my decision is. After having heard both sides and spending time with the child, I will have to rule to ensure that the best interest of the child is in favor with the respondent's requests. The child is to be transferred to its custodial guardian within two days. This is the court's final order," said the judge as he slammed down the gavel.

After the judge's decision was spoken Erica wrapped her arms around me and hugged me tight. Mark put his hand on my shoulder and squeezed it. Ms. Barker and Ms. Marcus helped Tur off the bench and walked him over to me. I grabbed him in my arms and kissed him. We thanked the court. Aton and Rona stood silent and watched the happiness that radiated from my side of the room. I took Tur by the hand and walked him out of the courtroom with Erica and Mark.

"We will meet you at your house," I said to Erica.

I then turned to Mark.

"Wait for me in the car. I will be there shortly."

"Congratulations," said Mark and left.

Turning around I went back into the courtroom. Aton was consoling Rona who was crying at the small table with her head in her hands as she clutched a balled up tissue. I first went over to Brian who was standing with Ms. Barker, Ms. Marcus and Jeanine. Lavonda was talking to Judge Lamb. I once again thanked them for everything and looked directly at Brian.

"Can I talk with you?"

Both of us walked away.

"I just wanted to say thank you."

"No need to thank me. Sometimes things may not seem as they appear and even if they are, what is more important is that one does the right thing. Besides, I just told Ms. Barker that you offered me an *Altoid* the night of the incident. I think they made the right recommendation and the judge the right decision."

Nodding my head Brian put his hand on my shoulder and squeezed it then left. I then knew he wanted what Mark now had.

I followed behind him and stopped at the small table where Aton was consoling Rona. She looked at me without a word then walked off. Aton caught up to her and wrapped his arm around her.

"Rona wait!"

She stopped and turns back around.

"I will need your help to teach Tur the canon! Will you help?" I asked.

Aton and Rona smiled at me.

"Yes, we will help," she says nodding her head. She turned around and walked off under Aton's arm.

# Chapter X

## The Perfect Mate

Rona had the perfect mate. Aton stood by her all those years and together they created a child who was in search of his own. I believe Stacy like his mother had found his in me. Unfortunately he was plucked from God's playground sooner than later. Nine months had come to pass and it was a hot July afternoon. Mark and I invited Erica and Leo to join us in taking Tur to see the new male bull that was born as a result of the insemination we had witnessed.

The five of us walked through the zoo heading to the moose exhibit, stopping along the way to see other animals as Tur ran up to different cages. As we drew closer to the moose exhibit, the purpose of our visit, Tur could see a moose off in the distance and went running for the fence.

"Moose!"

Mark smiled as we looked at each other and watched Tur. I smiled back.

"Tur wait up!" I shouted in consideration of Erica whose belly was about a foot out in front of her and Leo whose turn it was to carry the picnic basket.

As we drew near, Tur's face was pressed up against the fence. There were pink indentations on his face from all the previous animals we had seen. I grabbed him by the hand and pulled him back from the fence and lifted him up in my arms and held him.

"You're a big boy. Papa can't carry you any longer."

Mark saw me struggling to keep him up.

"Let me get him," he said and lifted him out of my arms and up above his head and over his shoulders.

"How is that?"

"Can you see?" I asked.

"Yes!"

Erica and Leo caught up to us. In front of the fence were a large tree and two picnic tables. Erica walked up beside us and held onto the fence. She took in a deep breath.

"This is a nice spot."

"Yeah, it's beautiful. The animals have so much room to explore."

Leo chose one of the picnic tables and sat the basket down. Erica took a quick look at the moose then sat down beside Leo and watched from afar. There was a family of three. A large bull moose standing off in the distance under a large oak while a female cow was standing in the middle of the field. Beside her was a newborn calve. It was eighty five degrees.

"Come here moose!" shouted Tur.

"There trying to stay cool."

"They are not used to this climate. They're more accustomed to cooler temperatures," said Mark.

Two sets of sprinklers turned on. The female cow jetted for the sprinkler with the baby calf and began to romp in the water. Erica watched from the table.

"That's adorable," said Erica as Leo smiled at her.

The baby moose hopped around the gushing water trying to drink from it.

"Look, he's playing!" laughed Tur.

Even in the sun, I could see Mark radiate. His glow was not outshined by the sun.

"What's his name?" asked Tur.

"*L'orignal*," I said choking back, "*L'orignal.*"

I did not have to think twice. Mark turned to me.

"Are you OK?"

"Yeah, I'm alright."

"How do you know that name?"

"It just came to me."

"Did you know that is what the French Canadians call the moose? It literally translates to 'The Moose.'"

"Yes," I said as a tear streaked down my face as I watched the baby calve play.

"Are you sure you're alright?"

"Yes," I said and walked away.

On the corner of the fence was a suggestion box to help name the new calve. Beside it was a pad and pen attached to the fence. I pulled a sheet of paper off the pad and wrote *l'orignal*'s name out and provided my name and address as requested. There were also brochures about how to adopt one of the zoo animals. I pulled a pamphlet out of the holder and folded it up and placed it in my pocket. Leo was holding Erica's hand when I walked up to the table and took a seat with them. For the rest of the afternoon we sat at the table enjoying our lunch. Mark filled in Erica and Leo on *l'orignal*'s story and how the semen was extracted and implanted into the cow.

"I think that's the easy part," said Leo.

"You got that right," said Erica.

Leo turned to me.

"We're going to need your help when the baby comes."

"Anytime, just let me know when. Both of you have been there for me," I said.

Erica started to pack up the leftovers from lunch.

"The zoo will be closing soon," said Mark.

"Yeah we better get going," I said.

Tur was still up against the fence watching the baby calve run around its mother.

"C'mon we got to get going!" I shouted to him.

Tur turned to us with disappointment on his face.

"Let's go!" I shouted.

Tur came running over to us. It was Mark's turn to carry the basket. I grabbed onto Tur's hand as we made our way to the exit.

"Can we come back?" asked Tur.

"Yes, next year," I said "How would you like to adopt the baby moose?"

"Oh boy!"

"You like that idea?"

"Can I play with the moose?"

"We'll see," I said as we left the zoo.

Mark and I said our goodbyes to Erica and Leo and headed home.

~ ~ ~ ~

Later that evening I sat with Mark and Tur in the living room.

"When can I play with the moose?" asked Tur.

"Why do you ask?"

"Because."

"That's not an answer," I said as Tur looked up at me and smiled with slight embarrassment twisting his body to the side away from me.

"You can tell me."

"I don't have anyone to play with me."

Mark and I both looked at each other.

"Not even in school?"

"No, the boys tell me I should play with the girls."

"That's OK. You know why?"

"Why?"

"I'm going to show you how to make a man. You can take him where ever you go." I said as I got up to go into his room to get some paper and colored markers.

"How are we going to do that?" shouted Tur.

"You'll see!"

When I returned Mark and I sat with Tur on the floor as I showed him how to make his perfect playmate.

"Let's start with the head," I said.

Tur picked out the black marker and drew a perfect round circle. I instructed him to fill it in with what he desired. Tur filled the circle in completely with the black marker.

"You're supposed to write what you want on the inside," I said.

"I will write it there," said Tur as he pointed outside the circle.

"What do you want?"

"Papa Stacy back," said Tur.

I took in a deep breath and looked up at Mark.

"Then write papa Stacy there," I said pointing to the side of the circle.

Just as Ms. Green guided Stacy years back I instructed Tur on his creation.

"You can draw the body next."

Tur dropped the black crayon and picked out a pink one.

"Draw the body," I said.

Tur drew an inverted pink triangle and filled it in.

"Now, what would you like in your playmate?"

"I don't know?"

"That's OK, finish making your man."

I turned to Mark as he watched Tur draw.

"What do you see?" I asked.

"Silence equals death?"

After our exercise, Tur picked up his creation and went into his bedroom. Mark and I also got up from the floor to get ready for bed.

"I'll be in soon after I tuck him in and he falls asleep."

Mark went into our bedroom. It was a long day in the sun. Tur fell sound asleep as soon as he hit the pillow. As he gently snored I walked over to the desk and sat down to continue writing where I had left off occasionally glancing up at *l'orignal* out of the corner of my eye. Mark put on Artie Shaw's 1940's version of *Everything is Jumping*. The music softly flowed into Tur's room and when the song ended my Geisha moose called.

"Come to Bed!"

# Epilogue

I don't know if this work would be something else if Stacy had finished it himself. I could only put forth what I believed what Stacy meant about creation and what he wanted to tell Tur about the rut. I used Stacy's technique of writing by documenting our life as it evolved. We never heard from Claudia. Tur spends a lot of time with Erica, Leo and their son named Staci, spelled with an I. Tur does get to see Rona on occasion. She has taught him an interpretation of the Jewish Canon that embraces same sex relationships. As he grows I believe he understands that he is being parented and raised by a gay male couple. How having two male parents will affect his future development, I do not know. Only time will tell. It's been a while since I visited the cemetery. Every year the anniversary of Stacy's death is remembered by visiting *l'orignal*. I'm trying to teach Tur the celebration of life and the act of forgiveness so that he learns, as I have, to make peace. If nothing else, I hope to instill in him the desire to engage in the most important act of God, creation. If this is something he does not choose to do with the rib of Adam, then I only hope that he carries the man he made with Mark and I that evening to find his perfect playmate or better yet, someone who will share his life journey. If not, he will always have the rut to frolic until his time comes and God plucks him from the playground of abundance he has provided.

# About the Author

Bernard Amador is the author of the memoir/screenplay *To Know A Fallen Angel: Understanding the Mind of a Sexual Predator,* the novel/screenplay *Cyber-Eugenics: The Neural Code,* and the screenplay *Used Books.* He is the Supervising Crime Victim Caseworker for the Albany County Crime Victim and Sexual Violence Center and currently a Doctoral Candidate at Northcentral University. He holds an M.A. in Forensic Psychology from Sage Graduate School, a B.A. in Forensic Psychology from the John Jay College of Criminal Justice, and a B.A. in Philosophy from Purchase College. He interned with the Domestic Violence and Child Abuse Bureau of the U.S. District Attorney's Office in White Plains, New York, at the Mental Health Association of New York, and worked as a Forensic Case Manager with a criminal justice agency. He lives in New York City and upstate New York. Visit him at http://www.toknowafallenangel.com